Hallmark
PUBLISHING

✳ *Christmas* ✳
IN EVERGREEN:
Bells Are Ringing

Based on the Hallmark Channel Original Movie

LACEY BAKER
USA TODAY BESTSELLING AUTHOR

Prologue

"Once upon a time…well, fourth upon a time, way up north in the tiny town of Evergreen, Vermont, there lived—"

"There lived a woman who loved Christmas very, very, very much," Hannah chimed in as she crossed the carpeted floor of the Evergreen Library's reading room to stand next to Nick.

Nick's boisterous laughter erupted. "Well, if it isn't Hannah Turner." He glanced at Hannah and then out to the dozen or so people sitting in rows of chairs. Nick greeted tour groups weekly, and this one seemed captivated by his snowy white hair and full beard. His appearance along with that signature laugh made Nick the perfect spokesperson for a Christmas town such as Evergreen. "You've lived in Evergreen all your life, Hannah…why don't you tell us a story about some of the people here?" he continued.

"Thanks, Nick," she replied, and tapped a finger to her chin. There were so many people in Evergreen whom she loved and admired, and the list of stories she could tell…well, Hannah's busy schedule wouldn't allow for her to stay that long. "Now then, I've lived in Evergreen all my life. I've seen people come and go. Our town vet, Allie, for example. She met her husband Ryan and her stepdaughter Zoe here." Clasping her hands in front of her now, Hannah smiled out to the interested bunch whose attention was now focused on her.

"A while ago, I watched my friend Lisa rediscover the magic of Evergreen, and then she bought Daisy's general store and fell for Kevin Miller." Hannah couldn't help but sigh at that lovely memory. "And yes, I was here when journalist Katie Connell met her match at the library and landed the story of her life with Ben Baxter. And as if that wasn't miracle enough that Christmas, my brother Thomas proposed to my good friend, Michelle, right there in front of everyone at the Evergreen Christmas Festival."

Not to fall too deeply into the memories without acknowledging some good points for herself, Hannah continued, "And I've had a few stories of my own. I wished on the snow globe for someone and…I found someone. I fell in love with my other best friend, Elliot. I guess you know what Christmas does to people around here."

Once she put it like that, Hannah tilted her head and recalled all the times she'd wished on that snow globe, only to have none of those wishes come true. Or at least she hadn't noticed that any had come true, not until Elliot. And boy, hadn't that still come as a complete shock to her? Who would've thought after all the years she'd known Elliot, and how much time they'd spent together at her parents' Tinker Shop, that one day they'd look at each other and see something totally new, refreshing and spectacular?

Trembling at the feelings that thinking about her romance with Elliot routinely brought, Hannah cleared her throat and smiled at Nick. "Anyway, this story starts with the Evergreen Christmas Museum. It's the story of…well, of my Christmas in Evergreen."

Chapter One

$\mathcal{E}$lliot Lee smiled while standing in the Tinker Shop. Through the window he saw a light snow falling, covering the streets of Evergreen. Inside, amidst white beadboard walls and laminate countertops, the ornament-making class had just ended.

Adding craft classes to the Tinker Shop had been Hannah's idea, but Elliot had immediately approved. Welcoming the town inside the shop he'd purchased from the Turners, one of the oldest families in Evergreen, had been a stroke of genius. And if doing so had brought him just a little closer to Hannah, then he'd take that as a win too. In fact, anything that concerned him and Hannah was a total bonus for Elliot. How long had he dreamed of their becoming a couple? The years seemed to meld together as he watched her now, wearing dark jeans and a gray-and-white-checked sweater. Her hair was styled in long thin braids. Everything about her seemed the same as the young girl he'd fallen for when he'd first come to Evergreen as a ten-year-old boy—her quick laugh, the way her smile lit up her russet brown eyes, her eagerness to help any and everyone she possibly could. But then there were some differences now that they were a couple, or rather now that he'd finally admitted he was in love with her. Those differences started with his desire to do whatever he could to make her happy. With that thought, his mind circled back to the big thing he needed to tell Hannah, the thing that Elliot was certain would complete both their dreams and push them toward a new life together.

"That looks great," Hannah said to one of the students, her voice snapping him out of his private musings. "I can't wait to see what you do next week when we try making wreaths."

The class began packing up the supplies they'd been using to decorate ornaments.

"And don't forget to sign up if you're interested in our art of gift wrapping class. Presentation is key to a good gift!" he said as some of the students stood and put on their coats.

"Bye, guys!" Hannah waved at a few of the students heading for the door. She stood at the end of one of the wood-topped islands smiling down at the leftover supplies—glitter, glue, plain white bulbs and more. "I don't think my parents could have even imagined what this space has turned into. You've made it into something the community just loves," she said, and paused again to wave and say goodbye to the last students exiting the Tinker Shop.

Elliot was proud of the place as well; proud of all that he'd been able to accomplish in this town where he'd lived since he was ten years old. Hannah, on the other hand, had been here all her life, and so she had an even closer connection to Evergreen. Still, Elliot felt as if spending his teenage years here still made him a prominent citizen of the town. Right after high school, he'd left to attend college, and to see what the rest of the world had to offer. But he hadn't had a moment's hesitation to return to Evergreen when his mother became ill. Evergreen was a good place and the Tinker Shop had not only become a good investment, but had also started to feel like a part of him.

"This is exactly what they would've wanted," Hannah continued as she moved behind the island, reaching down to the drawers on the back side to begin cleaning up.

Elliot loved hearing her approval and the thought that her parents would've approved as well. He'd had the chance to get to know Isaac and Barbara Turner, and knew they were terrific people. They'd also produced one amazing daughter. "Couldn't have done it without you, because someone had to carry on the Turner name," he said.

When she tilted her head and smiled at him, Elliot's chest swelled with the love he'd had for this woman since he was in high school. Of course, she hadn't looked at him as boyfriend material back then, but luckily, he prided himself on being a patient man. And eventually, well, last year at Christmastime to be exact, their time to be together had finally come.

"Well, looks like we're gonna need more space in here

now that we've added repair and restoration services," Henry said, coming into the back room of the Tinker Shop where they hosted their classes.

Henry Miller, with his stocky build and lightly gray streaked brown hair, had been working the front of the store while they ran the ornament-making class. Now, he grabbed his hat and coat off the coat rack and prepared to leave.

Elliot leaned on the counter where Hannah worked, folding his arms over his chest. "Imagine what we could do with a bigger space," he said, and glanced back to see her putting the unused bulbs into a box.

"Oh, yeah, imagine that." Henry agreed.

Elliot already had. In fact, he'd imagined it in great detail that he'd summed up into a five-page business plan. A plan he'd been trying to find the right time to discuss with Hannah. Now clearly wasn't that time, since she hadn't even responded to his comment. Maybe she hadn't heard him. Hannah was known for getting lost in her own thoughts, especially when those thoughts circled around her extremely busy schedule. Between her job at the inn, directing the choir, helping out here at the Tinker Shop and the other things she was asked or volunteered to do, there was barely enough time for him in her life. How did he expect to share this new plan he had with her?

"Thanks again for taking on the repair sessions," he told Henry. "I really had my hands full with the art lessons."

"Oh, no trouble at all," Henry said as he put on his

coat. "It's exciting to see how you've brought this place back to its roots."

"I didn't have much of a choice—the sign outside says 'Turner Tinker Shop,'" Elliot quoted.

Now, Hannah did join in the conversation. "Hey, I told you, you should change the name." She placed a few plastic bins she'd filled with clear bulbs on the shelves behind the counter.

That was true; she had suggested he change the name of the shop and he'd considered it. He just hadn't told her that part yet either. "People just keep bringing things for me to fix," Elliot said, trying to focus on the current conversation. He was well aware that there was another very important discussion that he and Hannah needed to have, whenever he found the time to make it happen. "Especially now that everyone found out that last year, I fixed the snow globe." He winked at Hannah. She'd been so upset about breaking Evergreen's famous snow globe. Seeing her that distraught had made Elliot determined to get it fixed. It was important for both Hannah and the town. But the greatest reward had been seeing the smile on Hannah's face when it was complete. He'd never forget it, or the longing glance they'd each known was opening the door to their love that night.

To be fair, it hadn't been Hannah's fault that she'd bumped into Nick while holding the snow globe and the globe had slipped out of her hands and fallen to the floor. But watching her seem so torn up about it had compelled Elliot to offer to help fix it. He hadn't realized that after all his years of knowing and liking

Hannah and working at the Tinker Shop when her parents were alive that now such a traumatic incident would bring them together. Hannah had come by the shop every day after her shifts at Megan's Country Inn to help him fix the snow globe.

"That makes sense to me. The Turners, they could repair anything, but their real love was their art," Henry said, looking from Hannah and then back to Elliot. "They'd be proud of what you two have built."

Henry owned the Christmas tree farm. His wife, Ruth, before she passed away, had been the town's main event planner. His son, Kevin, had helped Lisa renovate Daisy's Country Store, which Lisa now owned. And Kevin was now working with Hannah's brother, Thomas, at the lumber mill Thomas had opened in Evergreen. That's how things worked in Evergreen: one family connected to another and another. When he was growing up, Elliot had felt like an outsider looking in on all the close-knit relationships. After returning to town as an adult and purchasing the Tinker Shop, he became connected to Hannah and her family, something he'd never imagined happening.

"Elliot built it," Hannah said. "I just…"

"Spend all your time here helping me." He turned to look at her, feeling that warmth spread throughout his chest as it always did when they were close.

Henry chuckled and waved before leaving. The bells above the door jingled with his departure.

"Hey, I told you, you should change the name. My parents wouldn't have minded." Hannah came around to the other side of the counter where he stood. "I mean, now that it's this hybrid art, repair, restoration shop. A multi-purpose space needs a..."

"Multipurpose name," Elliot said from behind her, looking up as she mumbled the same thing.

"Exactly," she said.

"I've actually been giving that a lot of thought."

"Mm hmm." Hannah never stopped moving. She was always doing something, not content to remain still for long. It was something that had appealed to him all these years: her energy and giving spirit. Lately, though, he'd begun thinking about what would happen if she didn't have so much to do all the time. How would that affect their relationship? If she weren't so busy doing everything for everyone in this town, if they could get away and just be Hannah and Elliot, in love and living their life together? What would that look like?

If all went well with his plans, they could have that and more. The business plan and the loan application he'd submitted were just the first steps. Opening a second Tinker Shop was Elliot's dream, but it wouldn't work without Hannah by his side. If only he could figure out how to tell her that.

He picked up the broom and began sweeping the floor, to keep his mind focused on the matter at hand.

The grandfather clock chimed at that moment and they both looked at it. It had belonged to Hezekiah Beacon, who'd run the Evergreen post office for forty-five years before his retirement. After he'd passed away, Hezekiah's grandchildren had brought the clock to the Tinker Shop to be fixed, but had never returned to town to claim it when it was done.

"Aren't you going to be late to meet Michelle and Carol before your shift at the Inn?" he asked. Remembering Hannah's schedule could be difficult sometimes, but it was the only way Elliot was ever able to plan any time to be with her.

"Yeah, well, I like hanging out here with you," she said with a pout.

"Hannah Turner," he replied, and walked over to stand behind her. "Are you flirtin' with me?"

Hannah grinned. "A thousand percent, yes I am."

Elliot put the broom aside and moved closer to where she stood with her back facing him. Placing his hands on her hips, he spun her around. "Come here," he said and pulled her in for a kiss.

This was all he'd ever really wanted: to be with Hannah. There'd been so many nights he'd dreamed of holding her in his arms this way, of making plans for a future with her, spending the rest of his life with her. And now, they were here and...she needed to be somewhere else.

"I got this. Go see your friends," he told her, because he knew that friends and family were very important to Hannah. It wasn't lost on him that Hannah's schedule could be making it even more difficult to find the right moment to talk about his plans with her. It was just one more reason for him to want this change for them so desperately. Of course, if he'd been bold enough to tell her there was a reason she needed to stay here and talk to him right now, she would've probably made him the priority, but Elliot wouldn't do that. He wouldn't stop her from doing what made her happy.

She didn't immediately move, but continued to stare at him as if she knew something else was going on. That moment quickly passed and Elliot mentally kicked himself for letting the opportunity slip away again.

"Don't forget," she said while putting on her coat, "We have decorating at the Inn later today."

He went back to his sweeping, this time because it was something to do, when he really didn't know what to do where Hannah and this news he was keeping from her was concerned. "I'll be there."

"Okay. Bye." She waved and Elliot watched her walk out the door.

For the next few moments, he simply stood there staring out the door, hearing those bells jingling. How many times had he watched her come in and out of this place, smiling, laughing, talking a mile a minute about whatever she planned to do next? More than he could remember.

And how many times had he missed the opportunity to tell her how he'd felt about her? Too many to make any kind of sense, until finally the snow globe debacle had seized the opportunity.

With a sigh, he leaned back against the counter wondering what it was about Hannah Turner that still kept him tied up in knots. And why, now, after they'd been dating for a year and had fallen head over heels in love with each other, did he still find it hard to talk to her about certain things?

His parents hadn't been the best communicators, which was the reason why their marriage had ended in divorce and Elliot's mother had moved him here, a town she'd visited when she was a girl. His mother had wanted to get away from the city and the life of importance his father had built there as a restaurant owner. All along, she'd wanted a simpler life, one where her family sat down together to dinner each night and her only child could grow up with friends and being part of a thriving community. His father had wanted bright lights and success, and somewhere along the line they'd forgotten to tell each other about their differing plans.

Elliot didn't want that to happen with Hannah. He had to tell her about his goals and dreams since they involved her. She was such a huge part of this plan he'd set in motion a few months ago and he was excited to share it with her, to hear what ideas she'd come up with to add to it. He knew that's what she'd do; it's exactly what had happened when he'd taken over the Tinker Shop, and he'd loved every second of her being right there by his side. So why had he just let her walk out the door without saying anything?

He had no clue, and when a group of carolers walked by singing "Jingle Bells," he began humming the tune as well. Diverting his mind to the festiveness of the season seemed like a smart idea for the moment as he continued to sweep the floor.

Chapter Two

Of there was one thing Hannah Turner loved, it was walking through the town of Evergreen. There was never a day where she'd see the same thing twice, even though the town wasn't that big. And during the Christmas season, since Evergreen was known as a Christmas town, there were even more delights for her to spy while out walking.

Today was an especially nice day, with the streets lightly lined with snow and Christmas carols playing through the loudspeakers in the Town Square. People—citizens of the town mixed with tourists—filled the sidewalks in their hurry to get into one of the quaint little shops along the square or one of the lovely restaurants that all served delicious holiday-themed dishes.

"Hi, Mrs. Pringle," she said with a wave as the older woman came out of Daisy's and climbed into her car.

"Hey, Hannah. You almost ready for the wedding? I hear it's going to be the event of the year."

"Almost," Hannah replied.

Her brother Thomas was marrying Michelle Lansing,

who was the first Black woman to be elected mayor of Evergreen, and one of Hannah's closest friends. Michelle had been planning this wedding all year and on December 23rd, she was going to become Hannah's sister-in-law. Hannah was just as excited about the event as Michelle was. She couldn't wait to wear the beautiful silver gown Michelle had picked out for her, or to stand at the altar of the church watching her brother marry the woman of his dreams. With that in mind, she needed to stop by the cleaners on her way home today to make sure her dress had been steamed and was ready to pick up. Then there was the bridal shower. She had no idea what Michelle's sister, Sonya, had planned. Since Sonya was the maid of honor, Hannah had tried to pull back from doing too much for the wedding, but Sonya didn't live in Evergreen, so it made more sense for Hannah to take care of it.

"Whoa," Hannah yelled when she bumped into someone. "Oh, Nick. Hi!"

"Well, hello there. Are you coming to mail a letter to Santa?" Nick, who always seemed to be around town, though she'd never known where he worked or lived, nodded down at the red mailbox marked "Letters for Santa."

"I'll get to it, I'm just late meeting—"

"Now remember where all that rushing about landed us last time," Nick warned.

Hannah smiled, noting the cheerful red plaid scarf Nick wore around his neck. "Oh, don't remind me, I still have nightmares about breaking the snow globe."

"Nonsense, that was on both of us. We broke it, and I'll disagree with anyone who says otherwise."

Hannah nodded. "Well, don't worry, I tiptoe by it every time now."

Nick chuckled, a boisterous full-bodied sound that always reminded Hannah of the jolly Santa character in the old Christmas cartoons she loved to watch. "It's easy to get caught up in all the festivities each day counting down," he said and inhaled deeply, looking around the Town Square decorated in all its Christmas splendor. "Evergreen has that spirit. Everyone helping out."

"My parents used to joke that Evergreen was the kind of place that people would help out even if you didn't need them to."

"They certainly made their mark on this town," he told her.

That comment made Hannah feel nothing but pride. How great was it to have everyone in town always talk about her parents with such respect, love and reverence. It still amazed her that she'd come from two such generous and talented people. She only wished she'd one day live up to the high standards they'd set.

While she was lost in her thoughts, Nick looked down at his watch. "Goodness, is that the time?"

Hadn't he just warned her about rushing?

"Good to see you, Nick!" Hannah yelled when Nick dashed off. "Bye!"

She picked up the pace heading toward the Kringle Kitchen, the most popular restaurant in town. Carol and Joe Shaw, a couple who might've been in their early sixties, owned the place; they'd also been best friends with Hannah's parents. The Kringle, as everyone in town lovingly called it, was also the home of Evergreen's famous snow globe—the one Hannah would not be touching again anytime soon.

"Oh, hi! Sorry I'm late, guys." Hannah waved at the table where Carol and Michelle, who was maybe ten years younger than Carol, both sat waiting for her. Michelle's hair was curly today, hanging down to her shoulders in that rich sandy-brown hue that Hannah loved. She wore a smart green and blue plaid jacket over a navy turtleneck, and she looked every inch the elected leader of Evergreen.

"Oh, no, you're not late at all," Carol said as Hannah walked by her, taking off her coat. "You want some apple cider?"

Hannah hung her coat on the back of the chair. "Yes. Please." She took a seat and scooted her chair close to the table, being sure not to knock anything over. In the middle of each table there were red jars with branches of holly. Alongside that was a sleigh-shaped napkin holder and reindeer salt and pepper shakers. They were just a small part of the many Christmas decorations at the Kringle that made the place so festive and welcoming.

"I just happened to use the recipe from the new Kringle Kitchen cookbook," Carol said proudly, flipping back a strand of straight blond hair. She wore a white blouse with ropes of pearls, and a royal blue sweater that accented her friendly blue eyes. "First printing arrived yesterday."

"Congratulations, Carol," Hannah said. "I can't wait to buy a copy."

"Thank you."

Hannah had spent countless hours in this restaurant, studying while she was in school, and planning out aspects of her various jobs as an adult. This place was like a second home to her; besides that, because of her parents' friendship with Carol and Joe, Hannah felt connected to them and everything they did.

"So, ladies, the secret to the cider is adding the syrup from the Maple Syrup Sugar Shack," Carol whispered conspiratorially.

Michelle narrowed her eyes and nodded. "There's gotta be a shorter way to that."

"I know, right?" Carol added with a chuckle.

Hannah joined in, laughing lightly, as Carol walked away to get the cider. "So, Michelle, your wedding. What's left to do? How can I help you?"

"Well, there's really not much left," Michelle said with a shake of her head.

"The key for me," Michelle continued, "is keeping it small."

Carol returned with their drinks just in time to chime in, "Uh, are you sure it's not too small?"

Hannah had been thinking the same thing, but she hadn't wanted to say it. After all, this was Michelle's wedding and she didn't want to overstep.

"Well," Michelle began. "That's what we wanted. We met around Christmas, fell in love around Christmas. We wanted our wedding to be around Christmas." She looked from Hannah back to Carol. "We don't want to get in the way of anybody's celebration, so a nice little ceremony on the 23rd, then we can spend our first Christmas together as husband and wife."

The collective "Aww" from Hannah and Carol was acknowledged by Michelle's smile. Thomas and Michelle really were a very cute couple. Hannah had been ecstatic when she'd first seen the sparks flying between them last year when Thomas and his son, David, had come home for Christmas. Then, when Thomas decided to open a branch of his company here, Hannah knew Michelle had been a big part of that decision. She'd forever be grateful to Michelle for bringing her brother back home.

"That's so nice," Hannah said. "You two are a perfect couple."

"So when does Thomas get back?" Carol asked while tossing a towel over her shoulder.

Hannah grabbed a napkin to wipe her hands before picking up her mug to take a sip of cider.

"As soon as he closes the logging camp for Christmas," Michelle replied. "He waits for all of his employees to leave safely."

Something Hannah knew her father had done on plenty of occasions when bad weather was brewing here in Evergreen. Closing the shop by himself and driving the fifteen minutes to their house, where her mother would be nervously waiting, was nothing to Isaac. As long as his staff was safe, he knew he'd be all right.

"Well, he'll be fine, and we will just focus on making sure that your family gets in," Carol said.

Michelle sighed. "Yeah, that's the other issue. My dad, Gordon. I don't know what's going on with him, but there's something he's not telling me." Shaking her head, she continued, "Every time I ask him about his travel plans, he says he's about to make them, but then he never gives me his itinerary."

Hannah stirred the two sticks of cinnamon inside her cider. "Oh, well, I'm sure he's just busy. I mean, he's not going to miss his daughter's wedding."

Carol nodded her agreement just as David walked up to the table. The sixteen-year-old looked so industrious in his red Kringle Kitchen apron, and so much like Thomas, with the same almond-brown complexion and close-cut black hair. David was usually only with Thomas every other Christmas, and in those years, Thomas would come home to Evergreen, as he had last year. But this year, because of Thomas's wedding, David's mother had allowed him to spend the two-week Christmas break here and Carol had given him a job at the Kringle, just as she did with most of the teenagers in town.

"Hey Aunt Hannah, can I get you anything? A peppermint hot chocolate? I'm getting pretty good at making them," David said.

"I'm sure you are," Hannah replied and held up the mug she'd just taken a sip from. "But I already have an apple cider." But then, watching the quick flash of disappointment on her nephew's face, she continued. "How about you make me a hot chocolate for our Christmas movie marathon tonight?"

"Deal," David said. "I've gotta get back to work now."

"Oh, I love that kid," Carol said as they all watched David walk away.

"He's a great kid," Hannah said. "Having him stay with me while Thomas is away has been the best time. And he talks to Thomas every night about this job."

"So sweet," Carol said. "Well, hey, I gotta go help out in the kitchen. I'll be back."

When she was gone, Hannah looked over at the book Michelle had open on the table.

"All white flowers and twinkle lights on frosted white tree branches, that sounds beautiful," she told her.

"I know, right?" Michelle beamed. "I wanted something simple, yet elegant. I've even decorated my whole house in sky blue, silver and white this year, so it'll match the wedding colors."

"Oh, Michelle, that was such a lovely idea." Hannah loved wedding planning almost as much as she loved Christmas. "It's so creative, I can definitely see myself trying to think of something a little bit out of the box for my wedding."

Oh no! Had she said that out loud? Michelle tilting her head to stare at her basically screamed that yes, she definitely had.

"You know, I was thinking about that the other day," Michelle said.

Hannah cleared her throat. "Thinking about what?" Because Hannah hadn't thought about it that much. Certainly not every day since Elliot had told her he loved her.

"About whether there'd be another Christmas proposal coming this year." Michelle shrugged. "I mean, this is Evergreen and we've been known to have some love connections during the season."

"No, no, I don't think…" She stopped, figuring that by the way Michelle continued to watch her, denial was probably useless. "What I mean is that it's not something that Elliot and I have discussed." And that was the truth: They'd never talked about marriage. Her conversations with Elliot mostly revolved around the Tinker Shop, new ideas for the Tinker Shop, what movies to watch and what to have for dinner. Funny how she hadn't realized that until just this moment.

"Well, we might just have to give Mr. Elliot a push," Michelle added with a smile.

"Please don't," Hannah insisted. "I wouldn't want him to do something just because somebody told him to do it. Maybe he's not ready for marriage." Should she find out? Having a family she could love and cherish in Evergreen was all she'd ever wanted. If it wasn't on Elliot's list of things to do, wouldn't it be better to know that sooner, rather than later?

"No, I'm not gonna be that blunt. I'm talking about something like maybe purposely aiming my bouquet at you during the toss. You catch it and the rest is history." Michelle sat back as if her idea was actually a brilliant one.

Hannah wasn't so sure, and her and Elliot's future was not what she'd come here to talk to Michelle about.

"Let's just focus on your wedding for now. Is there anything else you need me to do?"

Michelle didn't look like she welcomed the shift in subject, but with a slow shake of her head she continued, "Anyway, you're going to look stunning in your bridesmaid gown. Thank you so much for agreeing to be a part of this."

Hannah waved a hand. "Nonsense. There's no thanks necessary. Do you know how long I've wanted a sister? I mean, Thomas is a great big brother, after we got past those years of him pulling my pigtails and breaking my dolls." She laughed at the memory.

"He loves you so much."

Hannah wondered if Michelle knew her eyes lit up each time she talked about Thomas. "And I love him, which is only one reason why I'm so anxious for you to become my sister-in-law."

"Oh, really, what's the other reason?" Michelle grinned as she continued to flip through pages of the book.

Of course, her question was just a joke, but Hannah answered anyway. "You've been such a great inspiration since you moved to Evergreen. I know you came here to visit while you and Allie were in college together, but when you got here, you just blended in and after a while we all started to think of you as if you'd been here forever."

Michelle sighed. "I know. That's why I love this town so much. Everybody opened their arms to me when I moved here and started working as principal at the middle school. Then, when Ezra announced he was moving to Boston and Allie convinced me to run for mayor, the town voted me into office. I've never known a place like Evergreen before."

Hannah looked around. "There's definitely no place like home."

Now it was Michelle's turn to look at her watch. "Well, I hate to leave when I was the one who scheduled this meeting, but I have to get to an interview." She closed her planning book.

"An interview?" Hannah asked.

"Yeah," Michelle answered. "At the Evergreen Christmas Museum. I know I spearheaded it, but I don't want to be in charge permanently, so I'm looking to hire a manager to take over."

Hannah had been to the museum, or what had been started in the old building at the end of the Town Square. She wondered what it would end up looking like and what types of things would be on display. There were so many great parts of Evergreen to spotlight, in addition to all its Christmas splendor. But before she could ask, Michelle was getting up from her chair.

"Gotta go." She hurriedly grabbed her book and coat and rushed toward the door.

"Good to see you," Hannah yelled.

"You too," Michelle yelled back before heading out.

Hannah sat at the table alone, still thinking about the museum, when moments later, the cuckoo clock chimed.

"Oh, is that the time? I gotta get going too," Hannah

said, and began to get up, grabbing her coat.

Time waited for no one, as her father used to say.

Chapter Three

A few years ago, Meg had decided to open a bed and breakfast. Ryan, Allie's husband, and Zoe, his daughter, had actually been the very first guests. Since that time, tourists had steadily flocked to the Inn during their stays in Evergreen, making the place one of the local hot spots. Hannah had worked as a part-time clerk and computer guru since the opening, and today sat at her desk behind the check-in station listening as Meg welcomed yet another guest.

"So it's room number six and there's cookies, pretty much always, on that tray," Meg said to the lovely young woman who'd just checked in. "And welcome to Evergreen."

Looking up from her computer, Hannah watched Meg absently push her warm brown hair back behind one ear, revealing the small Christmas light earrings she wore today. Giving the guest her customary, yet genuine, smile, Meg pointed to the tray of cookies. The guest grinned in return as she selected a homemade chocolate chip cookie with red and green candy chips. When the guest waved at Meg and then Hannah, giving a salute with the hand that held her cookie and said, "Thanks," Hannah happily waved in return.

"Enjoy your stay," Hannah heard Meg say, but she'd already turned her attention back to her keyboard.

After Meg came over to her desk to hand Hannah a Post-it note with the guest's name on it, Hannah commented, "That makes a full house."

"We've been full since Thanksgiving," Meg added with an incredulous look on her face.

Hannah nodded. "And now, guests are pouring in for the opening of the Christmas Museum," she continued, and stood to walk a few feet to where a basket of red netting and other decorations sat.

"Exactly, we'll be full all the way through the new year," Meg continued. "This is our best year on record."

Hannah smiled. She loved seeing the success of the town flourish through her friends and their businesses. That was one of the reasons she did her best to help anyone who asked. Whatever would make Evergreen the best place to live and visit had always been a top priority for her. She had the basket of decorations in hand as she walked around the front desk. There were never enough Christmas decorations and she planned to add more wherever she could.

"And since this is our best year," Meg said from behind her now. "Christmas bonuses came early."

When Hannah turned back, it was to see Meg holding a white envelope with Hannah's name on it.

"Seriously?" she asked, and then walked back to

the desk. When Meg only nodded and smiled, Hannah tucked the basket under one arm and reached out to accept the envelope. "You didn't have to do that. Thank you."

"No. Thank you," Meg told her. "You keep this place running. The computer system you've built practically runs itself now. So really, thank you, Hannah."

Filled with joy and a sense of accomplishment that never failed to fuel her, Hannah smiled. After circling back to her desk to tuck the envelope in her purse, she headed across to the front room of the Inn.

There was a huge stone-front fireplace that was the rightful focal point of this space. The quaint stone bench in front of it had already been lined with pots of bright red poinsettias. The walls were painted an antique white that carried over into some of the decorations, including thick candelabras, platters that held pinecones, gold stars, and red, gold and white bulbs. White figurines of reindeer, snowmen and angels marched along the wide coffee table and end tables.

Christmas was everywhere, even down to the scent of fresh pine in the air. That came from the real trees Henry provided that were positioned throughout the first floor of the Inn, and the wreaths that hung on the doors. Hannah would always love that scent, as memories of it filtering throughout her childhood home came rushing to the surface. Her parents, just like most of the people of Evergreen, had loved Christmas, and Hannah had loved them.

At seven years old, Hannah had happily bounced into

the house behind her father. Isaac carried two stacked boxes from the garage, setting them down in the middle of the living room floor. She inhaled deeply, grinning at the smell of Christmas coming from the huge tree her father and Thomas had brought home from the Christmas tree farm. Carols played lightly through the stereo system. It was chilly outside, but inside the house felt toasty from the warm blaze in the fireplace. Through the archway she caught a glimpse of her mother sitting at the dining room table knitting, red, green and white yarn strewn across the table.

Ever the inquisitive child, Hannah went into the other room, sat at her mother's feet and lifted the strands of red yarn in her hands. "Whatcha makin', Mama?" She wrapped the excess yarn loosely over one wrist and then looped it onto the other.

Barbara had been humming as she worked. Hannah loved to hear her mother sing in the choir, but sometimes it felt just as good when she hummed the melody of a song instead. "Scarves to take over to the church. They'll be added to the baskets we're stuffing with socks and snacks and other household items to be passed out on Sunday."

"Who's gonna get the baskets?"

"Anyone who needs them," her mother replied, and Hannah moved her hands to allow some of the yarn to be easily swept up into her mother's next stitch.

"How come you gotta make all of them?"

"I don't have to, baby. I want to."

"But Daddy's gettin' the decorations out so we can

put them up. Don't you wanna help us?"

Barbara chuckled. "I will, but while he's bringing everything in, I can continue to work on these scarves. Then I'll help with decorating. After we're finished we'll have hot chocolate and some of those cookie dough brownies you love so much. Then it'll be bedtime for you and I'll get these scarves finished before I go to sleep."

The smile had already spread across Hannah's face. She'd eaten all the green beans on her plate at dinner, even though they weren't her favorites, so she'd been promised a big dessert. Thomas had sneered at her because he didn't really like green beans either, but Daddy said he needed them to grow up big and strong so he could carry heavy boxes out of the garage too.

"I can stay up and help you with the scarves, Mama. Tomorrow's Saturday so there's no school." If her mother could sacrifice sleep to help the people who needed scarves, Hannah could too.

"Thank you, baby. That's very kind and helpful of you. But I'll be all right getting them finished alone. You need your rest so you'll be ready for your piano lessons with the Cooper sisters tomorrow morning."

Hannah didn't like playing the piano as much as the Cooper sisters liked giving piano lessons. "I could skip one lesson," she implored.

"No, you cannot," Barbara insisted. "You made a commitment, so you have to stick to it. Besides, you're getting better and before long you'll be playing for us in the choir. You've got lots of talent, Hannah, and I can't wait to see how you use it to bring joy to others."

The memory made Hannah smile as she stood rubbing her fingers over the spool of netting she'd lifted out of the basket of decorations. Even five years after her parents' deaths in a tragic car accident, she could still hear the words of encouragement they'd always spoken to her and Thomas, see their smiling faces and feel their presence in everything she did.

Humming "God Rest Ye Merry, Gentlemen," one of her mother's favorite songs, she continued moving around the room, twisting red netting around the pine garlands hanging on the mantel over the fireplace.

"Need some help?" Meg came up behind her to ask.

"Not really, I've got it. You go on and take a break," Hannah told her. "Besides, Elliot will be joining me soon."

"Ooooh, Elliot's coming over," Meg said with a mischievous wiggle of her brows. When Hannah blushed, Meg chuckled. "Okay, I'll go back to the kitchen to make sure we have more cookies coming out."

Alone again, Hannah was left to think about Elliot now. He'd been her best friend for so many years now, she'd lost count. They'd first met the winter after he moved to Evergreen. He'd been ten and she'd been nine. Friendship came so easily for them; she often wondered now why the love they shared had taken so long to blossom. Not that it mattered—she wasn't complaining. Elliot was everything she'd ever wanted in a man. He was kind and caring, hardworking like her father had been, compassionate like her mother, and he loved Evergreen as much as she did. He was, for lack of a better word, perfect, and Hannah was thankful every day that they'd been together this past year.

It was those memories of her parents and thoughts of her present and future with Elliot that kept her humming more Christmas carols as she continued to decorate. One day, she'd be decorating her and Elliot's home this way. That thought brought a huge grin to her face, a deliriously happy grin that she was glad Meg wasn't around to see.

It was late afternoon and Elliot had just flipped the *Closed* sign on the door of the Tinker Shop. Hannah was expecting him at Meg's in half an hour and he couldn't wait to see her.

Hadn't it always been like that for him? Since the first day he'd met her he'd looked forward to seeing her. That could perhaps be because she was one of the first children he'd opened up to in Evergreen. He and his mother had moved here the week before Thanksgiving break and had spent their first holiday alone in the old two-story house they'd lived in. Maggie Lee was a teacher and she'd started working at the elementary school soon after the break, but Elliot would be turning eleven that January, so he was already in middle school. Hannah was a year behind him so they hadn't met in school, but that first day he'd seen her outside the Cooper sisters' farm he'd known they were going to be friends.

It hadn't taken long for teenage Elliot to start seeing Hannah as something more. With a shake of his head at those memories now, Elliot moved to the counter where he kept his bag stashed beneath. Pulling it out, he grabbed his tablet from inside and turned it on.

Still thinking about Hannah and the days when he would come into the Tinker Shop just to see her. Of course, all the trinkets and gadgets had also caught his attention, and before he knew it Mr. Isaac had offered him a part-time job after school. It started out mostly as running errands alongside Thomas who was older than him by two years, but Elliot hadn't minded—it gave him something to do. Something he eventually grew good at. All that he knew about fixing things and running a business had come at the hands of Isaac Turner. Elliot's father didn't have much time to honor any real visitation schedule, which, after a while, Elliot hadn't minded at all.

Jack Lee had never been the type to spend time with his only son. Instead, the man who'd lived with Elliot and his mother in a high-rise apartment building in the city would be rushing to fix his tie, slip on his jacket and speed out of the apartment each morning. In the evening, after Elliot had been to the after-school program and then come home to finish up his homework and play a little before dinner, Jack rarely ever made it back in time to sit at the dinner table with them. But on Sunday afternoons, his father would relax on the couch and watch whatever sport was on television at the time and Elliot would sit next to him, relishing those small snatches of time with the parent he longed to know better. Once the divorce was final and they'd moved to Evergreen, Elliot had known—with a maturity he had no idea he wasn't supposed to possess—that the relationship between him and his father would only grow more distant. He'd accepted that for what it was—a truth that he could not change—and decided to move on.

But now that he was an adult, Elliot had his own relationship to worry about. He had the woman he'd loved for so long by his side, and wanted to do anything possible to keep her there. Glancing down at the document he'd pulled up, the business plan he'd worked on for weeks before it had been complete, he wondered if he might be wishing for too much.

"What's Hannah gonna think about this?"

He spoke into the silent space, as he'd done so many times since coming up with this idea. The answer never came, and he knew that was because nobody could answer that question but her. Still, a huge part of him was banking on her being just as excited as he was. She had to be; she'd been over the moon when he'd asked her and Thomas about buying the Tinker Shop from them after their parents' untimely deaths. While his father never made time to see him, Jack had provided financially for his son. And Elliot's mother had put all the money she hadn't used to help take care of him into a bank account that Elliot hadn't touched until he was twenty-five years old. That money had paid for the first step of his dream of owning a business.

Dragging his finger over the tablet, he gazed at all the pictures he'd sketched, the ideas for the next phase of his dream, and finally, the picture of him and Hannah.

It had been a whimsical drawing, something he'd just been toying with one night. He'd captured every detail of her lovely face, the mole just beneath her left ear, the tilt of her head when she laughed. It had been just in the past few months that he'd begun looking at that picture and wondering what it would be like to add more to it. A house in the city, nights out on the town, long walks in public parks, and eventually, kids. He grinned at the thought, warmth spreading through his chest as he allowed himself to revel in the idea of the future.

Now was definitely the time to tell Hannah everything. She was a big part of his plans for the next phase of his life and he wouldn't take the next steps without her. When he saw her, the next time they were alone, he was just going to say it, and then he'd hold his breath waiting for her response. That thought had his heart thumping in his chest right now. He needed her to be on board with this. Why wouldn't she be? They both loved the Tinker Shop and they'd enjoyed building it to what it was today. So there shouldn't be a problem. And she loved him. Elliot knew that without a doubt. His and Hannah's relationship was solid. They'd been friends first and had built on that foundation to form the love they now shared. They were good.

He nodded, feeling like he was trying to convince himself of those facts. Their personal relationship was just fine, even if they didn't spend as much time together as he sometimes wanted. But that was okay—Hannah had a lot on her plate. He understood that, had known it for years now, and it hadn't ever bothered him before.

But now?

When the old grandfather clock chimed, he jumped, knowing he'd taken too long reminiscing. Pushing the tablet back into his bag and grabbing his hat and coat, he left the Tinker Shop and hopped in his car for the drive over to Meg's.

It didn't take long to get there or to get inside the Inn, where Hannah put him to work in the front room.

"What?" he asked, while fixing a string of lights along the tree.

"You've got that look." Hannah paused momentarily and looked at him suspiciously. "Like that look you get when you need to tell me something but you're not sure it's the right time to tell me."

She was standing on the steps, hanging bulbs on the garland that had been twined around the banister. And apparently reading his mind. Not sure how he felt about that at the moment, Elliot cleared his throat. "Okay," he said, since he was evidently busted.

"Come on. Spill it. What's going on?" she prodded.

"I just keep thinking about the Tinker Shop. How it's become so many different things." He'd rehearsed that opening line all the way over here.

"Everybody loves it," she said with a nod as she reached to take another ornament out of the box sitting on the steps above her.

"I know, but now that it's getting busier and with Henry helping out, it feels a little bit cramped. I just keep thinking, like, what's next?" What was next for the business, or for them? For as much as he'd been thinking about this plan as the next step for the business, the "what's next" echoed in his mind with unexpected force.

Her silence wasn't making it any easier to digest.

Glancing over, he saw that she was completely absorbed with snow-topped sprig of holly. "Next, for what?" she asked absently.

"The Tinker Shop," he said by way of staying on topic, regardless of where his mind had begun to wander.

"Oh." She looked over at him and giggled. "Of course."

Elliot loved seeing her smile, and when she laughed, it relaxed him in a way that nothing else ever had. "I've come up with this pretty big idea about how to rebrand it. How to make it more about Evergreen. I've even applied to a foundation that gives funds to promising businesses." There, he'd said it, or at least part of it. Now, he watched for her reaction.

She paused what she was doing to look over at him again. "You did?"

"Yeah, see, Ezra told me about this opportunity—" The rest of Elliot's planned speech was stalled when a familiar voice yelled after the front door opened.

"Hello!"

"Speak of the Ezra," Hannah said, turning and coming down to greet him. "And the Ezra appears!"

Walking farther into the room, Evergreen's former mayor, Ezra Green, came in with arms open wide. He was a slim man with an easy smile and dark short-cropped hair.

"Hi!" Hannah continued as she went to him for a big hug.

"Oh, it's so good to have you back in town," Hannah told him when they broke apart.

"As if I would miss a Christmas in Evergreen," Ezra said, coming around to meet Elliot and giving him a hug as well. "Or Michelle's wedding."

"Welcome home, Ez," Elliot said, and went back across the room. As interruptions went, he guessed Ezra coming home for the holidays wasn't a totally bad one. Still, he would've liked to continue the conversation he was having with Hannah. While she hadn't said it, there'd been a hint of alarm in the way she looked at him, and Elliot had wanted time to tell her everything, to convince her that this was the right decision for them to make.

"Make yourself at home," Hannah told Ezra.

She picked up a plate of cookies from the coffee table and sat on the arm of a couch while offering it to him. Ezra, used to the Christmas treats at the Inn, happily took a cookie.

"I was just down at Daisy's General Store and they said you both were out here," Ezra said as he took a seat, and a bite of his cookie. "And oh, I saw some of those mugs that were made in the Tinker Shop."

"The art class made so many this year that we had to sell them," Elliot said. Hannah's knitting was fantastic, and the quick and thoughtful ideas she came up with to share that talent always amazed him. So much of their new creations at the Tinker Shop had spilled over into the town. It was just another reminder of how good the two of them were together.

"I recognized the handiwork on the little mittens attached to the handle," Ezra continued, giving Hannah a thumbs up. "Very cute."

Hannah beamed. "Thank you."

Elliot watched as she preened with pride at her work. They were such a good team, he only hoped that would continue after he'd had a chance to finish telling her about his idea.

"How's Boston treating you?" she asked Ezra.

Ezra's smile faltered. "Oh, uh, not easy. Everything changed right when I got there. I'm still looking for the right job that fits. And," he said taking a deep breath and releasing it slowly. "My relationship with Oliver didn't work out the way I'd hoped."

Hannah sighed. "Awww."

Elliot had spoken to Ezra many times throughout the past year he'd been gone, so he knew about some of the issues Ezra had encountered with his move to the city. Oliver, a retail consultant who helped companies design their stores, had first come to Evergreen with Lisa Palmer when she took on the task of saving Daisy's General Store. Of course, at the time, Ezra had been intent on selling the store, because there was no one in town to run it. As things tended to go in Evergreen, Lisa ended up reconnecting with her place in the town and she fell in love with Kevin. Ezra falling for Oliver had been another surprise development, and Elliot was saddened to hear that their relationship wasn't working out.

"But," Ezra continued, looking directly at Elliot.

"The energy in the city."

This too was something Elliot and Ezra had discussed, and Elliot felt a burst of hope at Ezra's words. This was the exact feeling he experienced each time he'd worked on the business plan and when he'd finally decided to apply for the loan from the foundation.

"And I know the exact right neighborhood for your second location if you get the funds you applied for," Ezra continued, before taking another bite of cookie and chewing.

That burst of hope deflated like a discarded balloon as Elliot met Hannah's quizzical gaze. The uncomfortable quiet that came as Ezra finished chewing his cookie and Hannah looked from Elliot to Ezra, then back to Elliot again, was palpable. Elliot could only sigh as the big news he'd been planning to share with Hannah had just been announced by someone else.

"What second location?" she asked Ezra.

With eyes going wide as if he'd just been caught peeking into a gift under the tree, Ezra stood. "Oh. I think I may've spoken out of turn." He cleared his throat, looking from Elliot to Hannah and then back to Elliot again. "Look, I'm just gonna go see what Megan is doing. And ah, let you guys ah…" In lieu of finishing that sentence Ezra bit into his cookie again before walking away.

"Thanks, Ez," Elliot said wryly before affixing a grin to his face. He ran a finger under the collar of his dress shirt that suddenly seemed too tight. This moment could go one of two ways, and he was hoping keeping a jovial attitude would help it go the way he wanted.

"So," Hannah began immediately after Ezra was gone. She looked equal parts confused and surprised and Elliot took a deep steadying breath. "If you get this money you've applied for what exactly are you going to do?"

He should backtrack a little, say something, anything, that would bring back the smile she'd had moments ago. Or, he could just spit it out. "I'm gonna open a second shop."

Hannah sat back on the couch. "Oh."

Her "Oh" wasn't the reaction he'd hoped for, and the exciting pitch he'd rehearsed on his way over here came funneling back to mind. "Bigger," he continued, exhilaration flooding him once again. "More services, even retail. I'm gonna have a platform for local artists to sell the things they make. All with that classic Evergreen feel. You know, the very thing that people come here for."

"But, in…Boston," she said with a nod that still didn't seem as agreeable as he'd hoped.

"Yeah," he replied after a moment's pause. His optimism bounced up and down as he juggled her reaction with the way he'd envisioned this conversation going in his mind.

"Huh." That wasn't a good sound.

"Yeah, but it's not just about setting up another shop." He pushed on. "I wanna do more. I kinda feel like sometimes, just sometimes, people see me as just 'that Tinker Shop guy.'" That part he hadn't planned to say, but it was the truth. He'd been feeling that way for quite some time now. "Like I'm only what I am because of where I am. Like I'm living in the shadow of who the town has always seen me as. Don't you ever feel that way?"

Hannah looked away like she was considering his words and trying to digest them. "No." She shook her head. "Not really. I like how the town sees us." She paused, frowned. "I think. You know, I've never really thought about it."

"I just feel like I'm barely scratching the surface of what I can achieve." When her brow was still furrowed, her lips unsmiling and she'd grown quiet, he stood. "But listen, we don't even know if I'm gonna get the money. It's all very cart before the horse," he said, and to keep himself from launching into a more adamant push for his idea, he picked up a reindeer statue from the table. "Sleigh before the reindeer," he said in a much lighter tone before shaking it in front of her.

Then he reached for her hand, helping her come to her feet. "We're in this together, Hannah. I want to build something big and special with you."

She came into his arms willingly, looking up at him in that way she had so many times before. "I thought we already had something special."

Suddenly everything Elliot had planned to say or do took second place to the warmth spreading throughout his chest. "We do," he said adamantly. "Oh, Hannah, darling, we definitely do. And like I said, we can talk about this more later, when I have more information."

Because right now the way she was looking and the hurt and questioning sound of her tone was more than Elliot had anticipated.

There was nothing wrong with what they had—he wanted her to know that without any doubt.

"We're fine," he said once more, this time lowering his forehead to touch hers. "We're just fine."

"Right," she whispered. "We're just fine."

But Elliot couldn't ignore the slight shift in the atmosphere around them.

Chapter Four

Today's schedule was a busy one for Hannah. That wasn't unusual; what was different about today was the curve ball Elliot had thrown her way. After he'd left the Inn, Hannah had managed to finish her shift without pausing to really contemplate their conversation. Now, as she walked through the Town Square again, this time on her way to the church for choir rehearsal, she let her mind roam free.

She supposed she should've asked him more about what he was thinking, but she'd felt so panicked by his announcement that she hadn't thought of all the things she was obviously thinking of now. What did he mean by wanting to open another Tinker Shop in Boston? Was he going to *move* to Boston? Dread and sadness swirled through her just as it had when she'd been sitting in the front room of the Inn with him half an hour ago. Why would he want to leave Evergreen? And when had he decided all this?

There were so many questions and not nearly enough answers. And to top that all off, Elliot had posed a question that she'd never asked herself before—*how did the people of Evergreen see her?*

Hannah had never given a thought to the way the people of the town saw her. She'd always seen herself as friendly, quick to help, anxious to please, and grateful for the opportunity to do all of the above. Was that so wrong? She had no clue, but she felt like she'd been thrown for a loop and she was still reeling. Even when she heard her name.

"Hannah!"

Hannah paused, right next to two potted trees decorated with multicolored lights. All the stores had decorations inside as well as on the outside, so it looked as if Christmas had spilled onto the streets of town. Just down the block there were giant nutcracker statues standing guard at the doorway of the card shop, and up ahead, in front of the Kringle, there were huge wreaths decorated with red, gold and green ornaments hanging from each of the three storefront windows. From around a massive multicolored decorated tree appeared her friend Allie Shaw—now Allie Bellamy.

With a squeal, Hannah ran to Allie and hugged her tight. "Oh, you made it!"

Over Allie's shoulder Hannah noticed a tall teenage girl with soft gray eyes and shoulder-length brown hair. This couldn't be Allie's stepdaughter, Zoe.

"Who could miss a Christmas in Evergreen?" Allie said when they broke apart, her smile a familiar balm to Hannah's frayed nerves.

"Zoe," Hannah said, leaning in to hug the lovely girl. "I haven't seen you since the wedding. Oh, where's Ryan?"

"He's flying in a little bit later," Allie said, as Zoe came back from the hug with Hannah to stand at her stepmother's side. "We came in early to surprise my parents, but they seem to be out."

"Oh, I'm gonna see them in a little bit at choir practice, but I'm sure they're somewhere around here." Then, because she needed to keep her mind on happier things instead of the alarming conversation she'd just had with Elliot, she turned to Zoe again.

"Zoe, so tell me: Do you love Paris? I know you love Paris, right?"

"Well, it's no Evergreen, but…it is Paris," Zoe replied with an exuberant laugh.

"So your nephew works here?" Allie asked, pointing to the Kringle Kitchen.

"David, yes, he just started," Hannah told her. "You know…" Hannah looked at Zoe. "It's an Evergreen rite of passage. All of our Christmas break jobs growing up were either at the Kringle or the Christmas tree farm."

Zoe shook her head. "Now you're making me feel like I want a Christmas break job."

And just like that, Hannah had an idea. "Well, you know, I could use a hand with the knitting. They sell my hats at Daisy's store and I make little mittens for some of the ornaments at the art center."

"Wait," Zoe said, her eyes wide with the thought. "Can I?" she asked Allie.

"Well, we have to go back to Paris in two weeks, but—" Allie shrugged.

"Oui! *Absolument*!" Zoe squealed her positive response.

Similar to the way Hannah had just been pulled from her thoughts by hearing her name called, Allie was momentarily jolted from their conversation.

"Allie?" Michelle yelled her name. "Allie!"

The moment Allie turned around, Michelle was there, grabbing her in a tight hug.

"Oh, Allie, I knew you would make it. I got worried. There was a storm forecast for up north so I thought they might cancel plane reservations," Michelle rambled.

"We would've snow-shoed," Allie told her. "We would've stolen a snowmobile."

"Zoe," Michelle said, and continued her remarks in French. "*Dites-moi la verité, a-t-elle appris le français?*"

Having taken Spanish as her second language in high school, Hannah had no idea what Michelle was saying.

Zoe obviously did and she nodded before replying, "*Elle s'ameliore! L'autre jour, dans un café, j'ai commandé un sandwich. Et un pull.*"

Allie, who seemed to be watching Michelle and Zoe carefully as they each spoke—trying to catch on, Hannah surmised—began to grin. "Something about a sweater. I don't know. You're the one who minored in French," Allie said to Michelle.

Michelle continued to grin and said to Zoe, "*Elle y arrivera!*"

"Yeah," Zoe said. "That's what I keep telling her, she'll get there."

The sound of a vehicle coming down the street caught Hannah's attention and she looked up to see a red truck easing to a stop across the street. In seconds, Joe and Carol were climbing out of the truck and running across the street.

"They're here!" Carol yelled.

Allie turned. "Oh, Daddy!" She ran to Joe for a tight hug.

"Zoe, come here!" Carol continued, going around her daughter and husband. "Come here. Oh, my beautiful girl. I missed you."

After their hug, Allie was up next and Carol pulled her in quickly. "And honey, oh sweetheart. All I wanted for Christmas this year was to have my family back here in Evergreen."

Hannah stood next to Michelle, cooing over the happy reunion. It was times like this that she missed her parents terribly. The big warm hugs she'd always received from her father whenever she saw him—even when it was multiple times in a day. The savory scents of her mother's cooking in the kitchen when she walked into the house. Seeing this reunion had her feeling especially nostalgic, and for the second time today she fought with the emotions swirling inside her. Her throat tightened as she fought to blink away tears.

"I wish I could stay," she said, her voice a little shaky as she looked at her watch. She was running late for choir rehearsal, but so were Joe and Carol.

Of course, as the choir director she should be there on time, but she still needed to stop by the Tinker Shop to pick up some music she'd left there this morning. Besides, the news from Elliot and this joyous family scene was pushing her to the brink, and the last thing she wanted was to break down crying in front of every-body because she couldn't get a handle on her emotions for some reason.

"But I gotta go," she continued, when Michelle looked over to her. "It's so good to see you, Allie and Zoe. I'll catch up with everyone later!" She waved and began walking, ignoring the quizzical gaze Michelle sent her way.

Hannah made it to the Evergreen Church, only fifteen minutes late for choir practice. She opened one of the heavy dark wood doors and stepped inside the sanctuary. A feeling of serenity immediately washed over her. The church always made her feel that way—calm, soothed, at peace. She only hoped it would last, but that was wishful thinking.

Seconds after stepping inside and seeing all the choir members already dressed in their robes and in the choir stand, Hannah picked up her pace, yelling out to them, "Hi everybody! Sorry I'm late!"

She felt like she'd said that a million times today and it was only a little after five in the evening. Rushing to take off her coat, she glanced quickly at the decorations that had been completed in the sanctuary. Warm white lights twinkled from the many wreaths and garlands hanging in the windows that lined both sides of the walls. Bouquets of white poinsettias were wrapped around the end of each pew with white satin ribbon. She'd passed a Christmas tree at the entrance; it was decorated in green bulbs with white bows and lights.

"Oh, we're just running up and down the scales," Jenny Cooper said, pushing her red-framed glasses up on her nose.

Her identical twin sister, Josie, wearing blue-framed glasses, chimed in behind her. "Keeping everybody on their toes."

The Cooper sisters were a mainstay in Evergreen, with their silver-gray hair, slender builds and penchant to speak in unison. Everybody who'd grown up in town had either gone to the sisters for music lessons or spent time on their farm helping out with the animals.

Today they were sitting behind the piano, where they could usually be found during choir rehearsal.

"A Christmas cookie," Josie began singing.

"Figgy pudding," the rest of the choir sang in return. They continued to sing while Hannah hung her coat over the back of a pew and picked up her bag, digging inside for the sheet music she'd run back to the Tinker Shop to pick up.

"All right," Hannah said. "Let's start with our…our opening number for the…" She paused, still digging in the bag that was now twisting with her ministrations. "The Christmas…ah…festival," she finally finished, growing agitated that she still hadn't found what she was looking for.

In the next seconds everything that was in the bag tumbled to the floor and Hannah groaned.

"Need a hand?" Carol said, coming up behind Hannah.

She hadn't seen Carol come in, but then again, she hadn't been paying attention to anything other than looking for the music that she was never going to find now amidst all the stuff strewn about the floor.

"Keep warming up guys; do more scales," Hannah instructed them, and settled down to clean up the mess she'd made. "Thank you. I have a lot on my mind," she told Carol, who had knelt down to help her.

As she was picking up the papers her mind circled around all that had happened today. She was a frazzled mess because of what Elliot had told her, and it was starting to show. "Carol," she said suddenly. "How does the town see me?"

Carol looked up. "What do you mean?"

"Earlier today, Elliot said this thing about how the town sees him, which made me really curious." It had made her more than curious, almost to the point of worry. What if, like Elliot had said, the town had this image of her that only correlated to who she was and where she lived?

"Well, we see you as wonderful," Carol told her.

On the surface that might've been construed as good, but not today and not at this moment. Hannah could only stare at Carol. What did her words really mean?

It must've been obvious that Hannah wasn't grasping that response, because Carol continued. "Okay. You do so much. In fact, sometimes, I think you do too much. You say yes to everything, honey. And then you run yourself ragged trying to get it all done."

Hannah's grin was slow and tentative because there

was truth to those words that didn't sound altogether complimentary. "Well, I feel like that's everyone in Evergreen. You know?"

"Well, we're helpful, sure," Carol said.

But Carol meant something else entirely when it came to Hannah. Hannah could tell by the cautious way she was looking at her.

"It's just with you, the job at the Inn, the art center, the Tinker Shop, the choir, any favor anybody asks. It's a lot." Carol's expression was meant to be soothing so Hannah doubted she had any idea how her ticking off all of Hannah's jobs around town had sounded like a list of negative traits instead.

"Well, you know, it seems all manageable." Hannah shrugged. "I see things I like doing, so I say yes." That made sense, right? Was being helpful such a bad thing? It couldn't be, her parents had been known for being the same way and everybody in Evergreen had loved them.

"So like your mama," Carol said, as if she could read Hannah's thoughts. "Barbara was always ready to help anyone she could, whenever she could. Sometimes I used to wonder when she took time to eat or sleep." A slow smile crept over Carol's face, but it seemed bittersweet.

Still, those words warmed Hannah's heart. Her mother had always been perfect in Hannah's eyes; being like her meant Hannah must be doing something right.

"Ambitious. Passionate. Caring," Carol continued. "That's how the town saw her. That's how we see you."

Well, that wasn't so bad. At least Hannah didn't think so. It was the way her parents had raised her to be. Besides that, she'd always given more of her thoughts and time to the people and the town of Evergreen. Considering how that made her look to those same people hadn't crossed her mind. It was the feeling that she was being helpful that had always taken precedence, until now.

"You're doing great." Carol rubbed her hands on Hannah's arms. "Just breathe."

To show that she'd heard every word Carol said and appreciated them, Hannah took a deep breath and let it out slowly. If her mind was still running rampant with thoughts and questions, then she'd just have to deal with it later.

"Just remember to ask for help if you need it. Nobody's going to think less of you if you do," Carol told her, and put a hand to her cheek.

"Okay," Hannah replied, leaning into the comforting touch. "Thank you."

When Carol walked away, Hannah whispered, "That's right. Breathe, Hannah. Breathe." She performed the action slowly, willing herself to focus on the present.

"Okay," she said again when she felt a little steadier. Turning around, she walked toward the altar where everyone now stood in the choir stand.

For the next two hours Hannah directed the choir through each of the songs they were slated to sing at the Christmas Festival and the Sunday services leading up to the holiday. Doing so kept her mind off all the things that had been worrying her today, and she let herself get lost in the music and the spirit of the holiday.

It was the best feeling, and it'd carried over as she left the church and headed home.

Hannah's car was an older model that she'd had since she was a teenager, so it was once again in the shop being repaired. While mostly everyone in Evergreen owned a car, often they preferred to walk from one place to another, especially during this time of year when the lights and decorations on the storefronts, buildings and houses were so beautiful to see.

It was while Hannah was walking home that she passed the turnabout at the Town Square and looked up to see the tentative sign in front of the building that was being transitioned into the Evergreen Christmas Museum.

The structure was built like a barn: honey-colored wood slats created an appealing visual. The green-painted steel roof added that Christmas flair, and even though it was later in the evening, the work crews were still buzzing around, wheeling crates and giant plastic snowmen through the front door.

It hit her slowly, the urge to go inside and see what had been added, but she had to meet Elliot and David for movie night, so she should keep walking. Her feet obviously didn't get the message, as Hannah stopped in front of the museum and just stared at the building for a few minutes more. The idea for a place to honor all of Evergreen's history and showcase its Christmas flavor had been a fantastic one and she'd told Michelle that from the start. Hannah was just as excited about the opening and the opportunity to see all the magnificent displays she'd imagined as the rest of the town. There was also something else that she couldn't quite put her finger on.

In the next instant, she was walking toward the door, stepping inside and looking around at the progress being made. So far, there were some lighted garlands already draped in places over more light-colored wood, cement floors, and boxes and tables covered with sheets. A partially completed life-sized version of the Kringle Kitchen had her gasping and then smiling.

Continuing farther inside, her mind whirling with so many thoughts about what else might be featured here, she stopped at a table with boxes on top. Inside one of the boxes was a lot of pictures. One in particular stood out. Hannah's fingers trembled as she picked up the photo of her parents standing in front of the Evergreen mural that they'd painted so long ago.

The horrible sensation of grief gripped her chest as the memory of the night Thomas had come to her room to tell her about the car accident flashed through her mind. She'd cried for days at the thought of never seeing the two most important people in her life again. It had taken her much longer to accept that they were gone and to move on with her life, and now that she'd thought she was in a good place, with all the things around her going well, there was this cloud of doubt. What was her real purpose in Evergreen? Was it really to duplicate the life her parents had led? Or was there something more in store for her?

"Hey," Michelle said, coming up behind Hannah.

"Michelle, this place is incredible." The words she'd been thinking for the last few minutes tumbled out.

"You know, when the town came up with all that money, opening this Christmas Museum in time for Christmas seemed right," Michelle said as they began to walk through the open space. "But now that it's ten days before our grand opening at the Christmas Festival, everywhere in town is booked. Lots of reporters are coming and I'm doing all this while planning a wedding."

"But on the bright side, we're gonna have a Christmas Museum." Hannah couldn't explain why that made her feel so happy right now. Even though she hadn't missed the worry in Michelle's voice, the energy of this place and all the possibilities dancing around in her mind were overriding any negative feelings.

"Look at you," she continued, reaching out to touch Michelle's shoulder. "Leaving your mark on Evergreen."

"While I am proud of being the first female mayor of Evergreen, I'm actually starting to think a little bit bigger."

Hannah had no idea what Michelle meant by "bigger," but she'd known Michelle long enough to feel confident that she'd achieve whatever she put her mind to. "Well, whatever it is, you've got my vote," Hannah told her.

"You know, I started this museum because I know that people come to Evergreen for how well we do Christmas. I think they should know the history."

Hannah had walked a couple steps ahead and picked up a small gingerbread house, holding it up to admire.

"It's gonna take a lot of work, though," Michelle continued.

"I thought you hired someone to manage the place," Hannah said absently, while still looking at the intricate design of the house—the drips of icing hanging from the rooftop and tiny candy canes painted along the perimeter like a picket fence.

Michelle sighed. "Yeah, I met with two candidates today. One took another job and the other…well, let's just say that was not a very organized person. Not at all. So if you have any suggestions…"

If Michelle said something after that, Hannah didn't hear it, because the idea that had just shot through her mind like a lightning bolt was already taking hold. "Actually," she began, a smile spreading slowly over her face.

"What about me?" Hannah asked, before she could let the thought take hold. There was a measure of fear that she might second-guess herself, considering the way her mind had been reeling today, so she smiled with glee at having said it first.

For a moment Michelle's eyes widened and she shook her head. "You?" she asked. "I mean, not like you couldn't do it, but really? This is something you'd like to add to your already very full plate?"

It was a fair question. Recollecting the way Carol had gone down her list of jobs a little earlier at the church came to mind. But she didn't care; this felt right. It felt…like destiny. "I want to do this, Michelle. Really. I already have so many ideas and I think…I think this position may be just what I need."

To prove a point, was the part she left out.

She did have a purpose in Evergreen, and something deep down inside her said that this was it.

"Look, you don't have to convince me." Michelle looked at her with a hint of a smile now. "I've known you for years, so I know what you're capable of. If you say this is something you want to do then, yeah, the job is yours."

Hannah couldn't explain how happy that made her. Instead she hurriedly hugged Michelle. "Thank you, thank you. I promise you won't be disappointed."

Chapter Five

As it turned out, Hannah hadn't been too late meeting up with David at the Kringle. He'd had some last-minute things to do and all the snacks he'd made for their movie night to pack up before he was ready to leave. So by the time she arrived, he'd just been coming out the front door, and they started on their walk home together.

They'd only taken a few steps down the street when Elliot came running up behind them.

"Okay, who's ready for movie night?" he asked, the jubilant tone of his voice matching Hannah's mood.

This was the first time she'd seen Elliot since their conversation at the Inn, so she hadn't been totally sure how either of them was going to act. There was no doubt there were still things they needed to talk about. For instance, why he'd planned something as big as opening another shop in the city without once mentioning it to her. But that wasn't going to happen tonight, not while David was with them. While Hannah desperately wanted answers from Elliot, she also didn't want to dull the excited vibe still buzzing around her newest endeavor.

"We are," Hannah answered. "David made us some hot cocoa."

"Oh, really? Let me give it a try." Elliot accepted the covered Mason jar from David and unscrewed the top so he could take a sip.

She noticed David's stressed look as Elliot tasted the cocoa, then smiled.

"Oh, that's incredible. You made this?" Elliot asked him.

David nodded. "I sure did. Carol says I'm getting better and better."

Hannah held up the bag David had handed her after coming out of the Kringle.

"He also made the best cookies I've ever eaten," she said.

"Joe even promised to teach me how to make the eggnog waffles. My dad's favorite." The excitement in David's tone almost matched the lightness Hannah felt about her news.

This felt perfect, walking down the street, sharing snacks and heading home to watch Christmas movies. For a moment she let herself imagine this was how it would be if she and Elliot had children. They'd take walks throughout town, enjoying the lights and decorations, and she and Elliot would share stories of their many Christmases in Evergreen. Like the year when it didn't snow in the month of November or three weeks into December and everyone was afraid they wouldn't have any snow for the holiday. She, Elliot and a few other kids from the high school had gone over to the next town and rented snow machines. They'd plugged them all in and, on the night scheduled for caroling at the Town Square, they turned on the machines with the intent to blow fake snow all over the town. But Huey Danfort had done some tinkering with the machine and the fluid you added to make it work, and instead of snow, the Town Square had filled with bubbles.

Hannah and Elliot had been horrified, for about ten seconds, until everyone in town began laughing, and soon they were all swatting at the bubbles and laughing just as if it were actual snow coming down.

Those had been good times, memories she would always cherish with Elliot. Would that be all she had left once he moved to Boston? *If* he moved to Boston?

They turned onto the walkway that led to her house. The house she'd lived in as a child and that she and Thomas now owned. Prior to this year Thomas hadn't stayed there much, as he was traveling for work. She usually only made up the bedrooms for him and David around Christmastime. This past year, since he'd been dating Michelle and opening the new lumber camp here in Evergreen, Thomas had been here more frequently. Still, he'd made a point of telling her that he planned to move into Michelle's house with her once they were married. So the Turner family home would be hers for as long as she wanted to live there.

The house was an American Colonial style with a wide porch and five front steps. White twinkle lights wrapped around the bushes pressing against the perimeter of the porch, while lighted gift boxes marched up each step. The pillars on the porch, front windows and the doors were all circled with lighted garlands, and big red bows were placed strategically for bursts of color. It had snowed a couple days ago, so a blanket of white covered the front lawn.

Elliot asked Hannah, "And how was your day?"

"Ah, exhausting," she replied, holding her Mason jar of cocoa and unable to stop the excited grin from sticking to her face.

"Really?" Elliot said as he stood by David now. "Because you seem—"

"Exhausted in a good way," she finished his sentence. "The way that's kind of exhilarating."

Elliot chuckled as if he were trying to relate to what she was saying. She didn't think he did, so she hurried to add, "I'll tell you later."

"Okay." His brow furrowed momentarily, but then Elliot quickly turned his attention to David. "So, what's it gonna be? Something funny? Christmas sad? Christmas somewhere in between?" With each question he jabbed playfully at David's arm, until David grinned.

"I'll find us a good one," David replied.

"All right, let's go." Elliot started to follow David up the steps, but Hannah stopped him.

"Hey, before you go in, I have some big news." "Later" was going to be now, because she couldn't hold it in any longer.

Turning back to look at her, Elliot paused momentarily before returning to stand in front of Hannah again. "Oh?"

"I got another job." The words burst from her mouth seconds after David disappeared into the house. When Elliot only laughed in response, she was so excited she laughed right along with him. "Yes! I was just standing in the museum with Michelle and I don't know, I felt so inspired by her, by the place, by all of it."

"Wow. But doesn't this put way more on your plate?"

Elliot was smiling, but his not-so-enthusiastic tone was disconcerting. "Well, yes it does," she replied and decided to keep going. Maybe once he knew the full story, he'd be as happy as she was. "But the thing is, today when you asked about how the town sees me, I gave it some good thought. And I was thinking Carol and Joe have the Kringle, Meg has the Inn, you have the Tinker Shop." She sighed and admitted something out loud for the first time in her life. "I've always felt like I've had these big shoes to fill and nothing to call my own, and then all of a sudden—" She snapped her fingers. "There it was. The museum. I can leave my mark at the museum."

There was a bit of a pause but Elliot's smile never wavered, so Hannah assumed he was simply trying to digest all that she'd said. She was still trying to take it all in herself so she didn't blame him, but there seemed to be something about the way he was staring at her, something she couldn't quite put her finger on.

"I'm proud of you," he finally replied.

"Really?" It was his tone that was still throwing her off. He'd continued to grin at her, but as she'd noted before, there was no celebration in his eyes or the way that he seemed to be just saying the bare minimum in response.

"Yeah." He nodded as if that action was going to be more convincing.

Hannah wasn't fooled. "But?"

"No. No but. Just, uh, good job," he said, and then touched his Mason jar to hers. "Good job," he repeated with the toast.

There was more to this, and Hannah suddenly guessed what it was. They'd both had news to share today and she supposed that earlier when he'd shared his, she might've been reacting in the same way he was to her right now. "Okay. So we can talk about the plans for the Tinker Shop if you want."

He nodded. "Yeah. Sounds like we both have a lot to look forward to."

"We absolutely do."

"So, um," he said and started up the steps. "Tonight, uh, Christmas movie with David's unbelievable cookies?"

His tone seemed a little lighter now and he turned to drop a quick kiss on her cheek before going into the house. She didn't have a chance to reply, not that she knew what to say at this point. It was better this way. There was no way she could question Elliot about why he wasn't excited about her news, without going into why she hadn't been thrilled about his. So he and David were right—tonight was movie night and that's what she planned to focus on.

Hannah's house was as familiar to Elliot as the little apartment where he lived. After selling his mother's house, he'd decided a smaller place was better for him. The Turner house was big, with four bedrooms upstairs and a garage that used to double as a space for Isaac to work on projects at home and park the old Cadillac he used to drive. Once Elliot had started working at the Tinker Shop in high school, he'd joined the Turners for dinner more times than he could count. While Hannah went to the kitchen to put the snacks David had made onto plates, and David had run upstairs to change out of his work clothes, Elliot moved into the living room to get the movies and TV ready.

Just a couple of weeks ago, he and Hannah had decorated the tree standing in the corner of the living room. He'd brought glass ornaments that he'd hand-painted at the Tinker Shop to add to all the ones she'd kept from her parents. Standing there now, he recalled that special night.

"These are lovely, Elliot! I can't believe you made them!" she'd exclaimed after unwrapping them.

One was covered in green glitter, with their names in a pretty script, and the words "First Christmas" and the date beneath it. The other one was red with a white heart, and their initials in the center, similar to the way someone might have carved it into a tree: "EL + HT 4ever."

"I wanted to commemorate our first Christmas together, as a couple," he'd told her.

"Oh, that's so sweet. What'd I ever do to deserve

such a loving guy as you?" She'd kissed him then, a light touch of their lips that never failed to make Elliot want to hold onto her forever.

She'd spun out of his arms quickly. Sometimes, that seemed like the only speed Hannah knew. And she'd placed the bulbs on the tree amidst all the other decorations.

Now, Elliot walked over to the tree, touching the red bulb. How long would he and Hannah's forever actually be?

She'd taken on yet another job here in Evergreen. How was he supposed to ask her to come to Boston with him now? Especially if she thought working at the museum was her purpose. And really, Elliot had no intention of stopping Hannah from doing or becoming anything she wanted. He'd just hoped that they would do those things together.

"What movies did you guys select?" Hannah asked, coming into the living room with the tray of cookies.

"Uh, David left a pile over there on the table," Elliot replied, dropping his hand from the bulb and turning away from the tree.

Hannah set the plate down and picked up the first movie from a pile. "*Home Alone*—oh, I love this one!" She was grinning so wildly Elliot couldn't help but smile too.

Minutes later when David came down to join them, Elliot put the movie into the Blu-ray player and he and Hannah sat on the couch while David sat with legs crossed on the floor closer to the screen.

"Kevin's such a cutie," Hannah said soon after the movie started. "I'd never leave any of *my* children if we went on a vacation. Then again, we'd never leave Evergreen at Christmastime."

She sat close to Elliot and he put an arm around her, hugging her close, but those last words she'd said rang loud and clear in his mind. Hannah felt like Evergreen was her home. Was it fair to even consider asking her to leave?

Chapter Six

"The Hat Factory was Evergreen's first industry. It opened in 1837 and closed thirty years ago," Michelle said the next day, as she and Hannah walked through the museum. She paused and looked down at her notes while Hannah scribbled on the pad attached to her clipboard.

"And the Cooper sisters just let the town have it?" Hannah asked.

"Well, yeah. I mean, it was just sitting empty. And when the town council approached them, they were happy to help."

Michelle stopped in front of a table full of framed and loose pictures. "Now, the hall of historical photographs still needs hanging." She jotted something in her notebook. "What we're going for here is a montage of photographs, all originals that tell the story of Evergreen's beginning years. There was land where there are now buildings, railroad tracks where there's now asphalt or cobblestone streets. I want to show everyone how far we've come."

Hannah sighed with the energy that buzzed in the air. "The old turning into the new," she said, more to herself than in response to Michelle's words.

"Exactly," Michelle replied.

"Hey, you two," Elliot said, coming up behind them. "I figured I'd stop by with a warmup and see how things are coming along. Or if there's anything I can do to help while Henry's taking care of the Tinker Shop?"

Hannah was happy to see him, although she wondered why he'd leave the Tinker Shop mid-morning to come help out here. He was holding a tray with two jars of hot cocoa, but all Hannah saw was his warm smile.

"Thanks, Elliot," Michelle said, helping herself to one of the jars and setting it on a side table. "I'm going to leave this right here and circle back for it when I get finished. I think we've got everything under control, but would you like a tour?"

"I'd love one," he replied, with a quick glance at Hannah.

He seemed to want her to say something, give her permission maybe. Tell him to go? She wasn't quite sure, so she stepped closer and took the other jar from the tray instead. Leaning in, she kissed him on the cheek before saying, "Thanks so much for coming."

It was what she felt, gratitude. Because whatever the reason he'd come to the museum today, she was happy to see him. Happy to know that they were still okay, even with the new developments between them.

"So we bought these screens to play old news footage that we had at the library. I also want to focus on the stories," Michelle said.

Hannah stepped into the space. There were black drapes along the walls here, a chair, and a podium with a half-decorated Christmas tree behind it. Michelle had pointed to the screens while she spoke and Elliot moved to go look behind them.

"History of the town," Hannah said, piggybacking off Michelle's comment with a nod. "I like that." Then, after a little more thought, she continued, "Maybe some of the townspeople would like to be interviewed. Then we could use those videos on the screens."

"Yes!" Michelle nodded. "See, this is why we needed you to come on board."

Michelle continued walking in front of them and when Hannah looked back, Elliot was giving her a thumbs-up signal.

"And then there's the gift shop," Michelle said, leading them into yet another room in the old factory. "People always love a good souvenir."

Hannah gazed around at the square footage, noting the small space with two white curio cabinets and a wall of built-ins. There were already a few things on the shelves—a couple of antique tea pots with poinsettia designs and a vintage bottle from the Maple Sugar Syrup Shack.

"Okay. Well, the Tinker Shop can definitely help with this part. For a place practically famed for its magical snow globe, I'm sure we can make a few for sale," she said, glancing over at Elliot.

"No doubt. You always have the best ideas, Hannah."

She met his smiling gaze with a quick grin of her own. "There's also the ornaments from the classes and so many other trinkets we could bring over," he continued.

Michelle chuckled. "That is a great idea. Any trinkets or ornaments you can spare."

"We could also keep pamphlets for the museum at the Tinker Shop too. That way we're cross-promoting each place, covering all our bases with tourists," Elliot added.

He had a great mind for business. That was something Hannah had noticed about him right away as he'd continued to work at the Tinker Shop during high school. Whenever her father and Thomas had stood around talking about displays or ways to increase traffic in the shop, Elliot had always been there with a new idea. It was no wonder he'd been ready to implement so many new features at the shop once he took over. And she'd thoroughly enjoyed being there with him, to chime in with her own thoughts and talents here and there.

Hannah scribbled the notes onto her pad; she didn't want to forget a thing. It was so easy working with Elliot right by her side and they seemed to slip easily into the groove of speaking about the Tinker Shop. That was something she didn't want to end—their partnership, whether business or personal, was very important to her.

"And there's one more thing," Michelle said, and turned away from them. "Follow me."

Hannah and Elliot walked behind her down a winding hallway, with more boxes and cloths covering mysterious objects. The smell of sawdust mixed with the fresh pine scent that had probably been sprayed all over the Christmas decorations already hanging around the place.

When Michelle stopped, Hannah noticed they were once again at the front entrance of the museum. Michelle stared up at the wall right across from the double doors. Hannah and Elliot came up behind her, staring as well.

"It's the first thing guests will see when they enter," Michelle said, nodding toward the picture on the wall. "Hiram Cooper, founder of the Hat Factory."

Hannah couldn't help but fix her face to match the frown on the man in the picture. "I wonder if he ever smiled." A man wearing such a spiffy top hat as Hiram wore in the gray-toned photograph should have a confident smile. The gold beveled-edge frame surrounding the photo was caked with dust and looked like a heavy antique.

"Well, he certainly didn't seem happy to be taking that picture," Elliot said.

"Right. Well, we're gonna need something else up there," Michelle told them.

"Just paint a Santa hat on the old grinch and call it a day," a voice from behind them said.

The threesome turned around to see a woman standing in the doorway.

"Sonya!" Michelle exclaimed, and ran to hug the woman.

"I've been looking all over for you," Sonya said when the hug broke. "Which isn't difficult given the size of this town."

Happily watching the exchange, Hannah realized this was Michelle's sister. Sonya was a few inches taller than Michelle, her hair styled in twists pulled up into a row of tight curls. She wore a rose-colored coat and black leather gloves, and had a sentimental look on her face that spoke of how happy she was to see her sister. Hannah had often wondered what it would've been like to have a sister. Now, through marriage, it looked like she'd be gaining two.

"Elliot, Hannah, this is my sister Sonya." Michelle happily introduced them.

Sonya waved and Hannah immediately replied, "Oh, it's so nice to finally meet you." She'd heard so much about Sonya from Michelle that she felt like she already knew her. Still, this was their first face-to-face and as was often the way of greeting in Evergreen, Hannah moved in to hug her.

"You too," Sonya said after stepping back from Hannah. "Michelle's told me so much about you."

"Well, welcome to Evergreen," Hannah replied.

"It's nice to meet you, Sonya. Welcome to Evergreen," Elliot said, and stepped up to shake Sonya's hand.

"How are you liking it here so far?" Hannah asked.

"It's cold," Sonya replied with a shiver.

Michelle shook her head. "Sonya lives in New Mexico, where the temperatures are warmer and the tempers are shorter."

Sonya grinned at her sister's remark. "It doesn't have all this holly and…" She paused and sniffed the air. "Is that cinnamon?"

Michelle playfully nudged her as she laughed. Hannah thought the contrast between them was interesting—Michelle loved Christmas, yet Sonya seemed indifferent to it. Hannah couldn't imagine not liking Christmas, and she sort of felt bad for Sonya, because in the next days she was going to be bombarded by any and everything holiday-related.

"But it's nice," Sonya continued, and turned her attention back to Hannah and Elliot.

"Are you all set with the list?" Michelle asked Hannah.

"Absolutely." To solidify that declaration, Hannah tapped her hand on the clipboard and nodded. "Don't you even think about it for another second. Just worry about your wedding."

"Thank you, Hannah," Michelle said. "Seriously, thank you."

And there it was right there, that hint of pleasure that came each time she did something for someone around Evergreen. So how could she be taking on too much, if with every task she felt so good? Hannah couldn't help that her mind kept circling back to the same point. She partially blamed Elliot for asking her that question about what people thought of her in the first place. For years she'd been happily moving along without ever wondering if there was something wrong with the way she was living her life.

Today, she was inclined to believe she was on the right track.

"So, you hungry?" Michelle asked her sister. "You

wanna go to the Kringle?"

"Sure," Sonya replied, but crinkled her nose. "Do they have anything other than gingerbread men?"

Michelle rolled her eyes and grinned before she looped her arm through Sonya's and led her out the door. Hannah watched as they left, then turned to face Elliot again.

"So, you about finished here for the day?" he asked her.

"Um, no, I think I want to do another walk around and take some more notes."

"I can stick around and help if you want."

She tilted her head, staring at him then. "Hey, Elliot, why'd you really stop by today? I mean, I know you have things going on at the Tinker Shop."

"Henry's there this morning," he replied with a shrug. "But I also wanted to come by and tell you that I support your decision to work here at the museum." He took a step closer, his brown eyes watching her in that way that made her feel as if she were the only woman in the world. "I mean, I get it, really I do. And if this makes you happy—if it puts that pretty smile on your face that I've been seeing since I've been here—then I'm all for it and I'll help you in any way I can."

If hearts could melt, Hannah's was now in a puddle at Elliot's feet. Oh, how she loved this man. All the doubts she'd been having since he'd mentioned opening the second Tinker Shop seemed to dissipate with his present words.

"Oh, Elliot. Thank you so much for saying that."

She wrapped her arms around his neck and pulled him to her for a hug so tight it could've been classified as crushing.

But Elliot never said a word; he simply hugged her back, holding her just as tightly as she felt she was holding him.

"Shall we head over to the General Store for supplies to help you get started here?" Elliot asked when they finally pulled away.

She thought about his offer for a second, mentally going over her full schedule for the day. "Oh, no, I have to do some things out at the Inn, then I have to deliver some hats to Daisy's store, and then, later, stop by the Cooper sisters' to pick up some more sheet music for the choir. So I won't have time to do another walk around here."

"Oh. Well, in that case, let me deliver the hats for you—that should free up some of your time, and—"

Touched, she shook her head. "Elliot, don't you have a class to teach at the Tinker Shop this afternoon?"

"I know, but I'd like to help you out if I can," he told her earnestly.

"Thank you. I really appreciate your wanting to help me. But I've got this," she said.

He nodded. "Okay, if you're sure. Then I'll meet you at your place tonight? Around seven?"

"Definitely," Hannah replied, already looking forward to the time she'd get to spend with Elliot alone.

"I just don't get it," Sonya said when she and Michelle were seated at the Kringle. "Why're there so many trees around here? There's one over there in the corner decorated in bright pink, turquoise and lime green bulbs—a color combo I've never seen on a Christmas tree, by the way." She chuckled and then continued. "And then there's another one over there with what looks like gingerbread men and their family exploded on it. There're two more trees outside the door, and—"

"How many times do I have to tell you, that's what we do best here in Evergreen?" Michelle asked.

Oh. how she'd missed her cynical, complaining sister. It'd been at least two years since Michelle had traveled to New Mexico to visit Sonya for her birthday. This was the first time in all the years Michelle had been in Evergreen that Sonya had agreed to come for a visit. Their mother wouldn't have been happy at how much time their family spent apart.

It had been ten years since Diana Lansing had passed away, and in that time, the distance between Michelle, Sonya and their father had grown more than just the miles that separated the different states they each lived in. Losing her mother had been hard on Michelle, but Sonya and Gordon had taken the loss much harder, both going to their separate corners of the world and deciding to sulk there. But Michelle was hoping that this year, her wedding could bring them all back together again.

She was so excited to see her sister Michelle couldn't help but smile. The plum-colored dress Sonya wore with split sleeves accented her sepia-hued complexion and added just another cheerful splash of color to the décor at the Kringle Kitchen—even though Michelle knew her sister wouldn't especially think that was a compliment.

"Anyway," Sonya continued. "Let's get to this wedding. We've got so much to do and so little time."

Michelle took a slow, steadying breath. From the tone of the emails she and Sonya had been exchanging over the last months, she knew what she was about to say might not go over too well. "I loved some of your wedding suggestions; it's just that they—" Michelle paused as Sonya slowly raised a brow. Then, thankfully, over her sister's shoulder she glimpsed David approaching. "Oh, the perfect hot cocoa," she said a little too enthusiastically, as he came up to the table and set down two mugs. "Just the right balance of chocolate to milk."

"Practice makes perfect," David replied.

"That's right," she said, and offered a fist bump. David had no idea she was also thanking him for the sweet interruption.

David tapped his fist to hers with a proud grin.

"You know," Sonya said to David. "Your dad is marrying my sister in a few days. I went all this time not being someone's auntie, but Michelle tells me you taught her how to ice skate. So, you wanna show me later?"

"Yeah, that'd be great," David told her.

For a few seconds Michelle marveled at what was soon going to be her family. She'd introduced Sonya to David when they first walked into the Kringle. Now her sister, whom she loved with all her heart, and her soon-to-be stepson, whom she wanted nothing but the very best for, were planning an outing together. The only way this could get any better would be if Thomas were here with them.

"Okay, I'm gonna hold you to that," Sonya said, and watched David walk away. "He's so cute," she continued with a grin. "Seems like a good kid."

"Mmm hmm," Michelle nodded. "And he's smart too. Thomas said he's already planning which college he'll attend and wants to study engineering. But with the way he's been baking and mixing these holiday drinks around here, I wouldn't be surprised if he switches to culinary."

Then Michelle pulled a candy cane from the jar on the table, unwrapped it and dropped it into Sonya's hot chocolate.

Sonya immediately looked down, then back up to Michelle with a frown.

"What are you doing?" Sonya asked.

Michelle stared down at her sister's mug to the medium-sized marshmallows drizzled with chocolate syrup on top. The candy cane actually added a nice dash of color to the drink. "It melts while you drink it and adds a festive little peppermint kick."

Sonya's face was deadpan.

"Ugh," Michelle said with a shake of her head, and reached over to remove the candy cane. "All right, more for me." She happily tucked the candy cane inside her own mug.

Sonya was still frowning when Michelle picked up her mug to take a quick sip. Noting that the interruption was over and that she needed to pick up where her conversation had left off with Sonya, she just jumped right in. "So, I really appreciate your wedding suggestions. It's just that—"

"It's your wedding day," Sonya implored. "You only get one. Well," she added with a tilt of her head. "Some people get more than one, but you know what I mean."

"A wedding is a union of love. Sure, the people and the party are fun, but we didn't want it to be over the top."

"A Christmas-themed wedding, and you're telling me that's not over the top." Sonya looked around, pointing at some of the decorations. "This whole town's over the top. It's like being trapped in a Christmas snow globe."

"Hey, hey, hey, I love this town, and if you and Daddy would ever come for Christmas you would actually love it too."

"My humble apologies, Madam Mayor." Sonya grinned and reached out to take Michelle's hand.

"I just wish Dad would commit to his travel plans," Michelle said.

Sonya pulled her hand away and rolled her eyes. "Yeah, well, good luck with that."

That remark was a little beyond Sonya's normal skepticism, and it only made Michelle more anxious. "What's that supposed to mean?" Michelle asked

"Nothing," Sonya replied with a shrug. "Let's get down to business about this wedding. Now, I've got to try on my gown and then, can we do something about adding some color to the winter wonderland scheme you've got going on? I actually think I'm starting to like that splash of pink on the tree over there."

Michelle shook her head. "We're not adding anything pink to my wedding," she told her sister, and decided not to worry about her father and his travels plans at the moment.

Right now, she was just going to enjoy this time in her favorite place with her favorite sister.

Chapter Seven

When Hannah arrived at the Cooper sisters' farm to pick up the sheet music for the choir, she paused at the sound of a piano playing. As a child she'd tried to take piano lessons from the sisters, but that hadn't gone well. Of all the talents she possessed, piano playing was not one of them.

The thought made her smile, and she was just about to knock on the door when she heard a familiar voice through the open window. Though it was cold outside, the Cooper sisters liked fresh air coming into their house at all times. Hannah had asked them about this a time or two when she'd been there and halfway freezing while she stood in their music room. The chilly breeze didn't seem to bother either of the sisters so Hannah had never asked again—it was their house, after all.

"That's good, David!" Josie said.

Hannah moved closer to the open window, leaning over to peek inside. David was sitting at the piano playing "O Holy Night." Hannah was shocked to see him sitting there. Since when had he been taking piano lessons? Thomas hadn't told her that, and neither had David. And he sounded *good*.

"Now, hurry up and get your coat on," Jenny told him. "Your Aunt Hannah's stopping by to pick up some music."

David stopped playing and turned on the bench to look at the sisters. "She's not the best at keeping surprises," he said, and Hannah frowned. "Especially from my dad."

What? She could keep a surprise! Couldn't she?

There'd been plenty of things she hadn't told Thomas growing up, like when her parents had gotten him that ten-speed bike he'd wanted. Hannah had seen it out in the garage under a green tarp her father had tossed over it. It was bright red with the hand brakes that Thomas had been wanting. Her brother was fifteen and Hannah had been eleven. She'd been in the garage looking for more art supplies for the decorations she was making for the Christmas pageant at school. Even back then, she'd always gotten in the spirit of helping out.

When Josie headed over to close the window, Hannah hurried out of the way, pressing her back against the wall so she wouldn't be seen. Figuring they were on their way out, she tiptoed over to the steps, meaning to go down and pretend to be coming up, but the door opened faster than expected and she turned around just in time to see her nephew walking out.

Stopping suddenly, David's eyes widened as he stared at her. "Aunt Hannah?"

She tried to play it off with what she hoped was a

nonchalant shrug. "David?"

The Cooper sisters stepped out onto the porch as well. Jenny—who wore a burgundy shirt beneath a charcoal-gray sweater and black skirt—stood next to David with a box in hand, sheet music on top of it.

While Josie, dressed in a full charcoal-gray sweater and black skirt to match her sister's, said from his other side, "He was just helping us decorate." She reached back and grabbed a table ornament to show Hannah.

"This lovely sled." Jenny followed up with a sly look at David.

Hannah glanced at the sled and then back to Jenny, who was a terrible liar.

"Yeah," David said, moving to take the sled from Josie. "For Christmas."

Because the ornaments and holly attached to the sled weren't a dead giveaway. Seems David wasn't any better at making up stories than the Cooper sisters were. They were quite a pair, with their hair styled identically in tight buns that sat happily on top of their heads.

"And here's your sheet music for the choir." Jenny jumped right in, handing the folder to Hannah. "We picked out a few more favorites and we even threw in some recordings of the old concerts." That was the box that Hannah immediately reached for.

"You recorded the choir back then?" she asked, having already pushed aside their excuses for why David was there.

"Oh, all the time; these recordings are just collecting dust."

"Wow." Hannah's mind was already reeling with a new idea. "Maybe we should play these at the Christmas Museum."

"Oh," the Cooper sisters replied in unison—as they often did—clapping their hands together in matching gestures. "Absolutely."

Hannah simply adored them and their always upbeat spirit. "Jenny and Josie, thank you so much for this."

"Oh, you're welcome," Josie said while Jenny smiled.

"So." Turning to David, Hannah asked, "You need a lift?"

Nodding and grinning, he replied, "Oh, uh, yeah."

"Okay, come on."

Hannah turned to walk down the steps, waving back at the Cooper sisters.

"Bye!" the Cooper sisters replied in a dual sing-songy voice.

More new developments. That's what Hannah thought on their way home. So many things were going on lately with the upcoming wedding, Elliot's announcement, her new job, and now David was apparently taking piano lessons. She certainly hadn't seen that coming, and truthfully, she wasn't quite sure what to make of it, but since it was a "surprise"—their words, not hers—she supposed she didn't actually have to think of it at all. What better way for her to prove she was good at keeping surprises, than for her not to thoroughly investigate the details of this one? The strange twist of events had her smiling as she drove along the quaintly decorated streets of Evergreen.

The house on Sycamore Road had been home for all of Hannah's life. Walking up onto the porch tonight, she paused for a second to take that in. She'd decorated out here herself, of course, not leaving one space free of garlands, lights, bulbs, bows or whatever other decorations she could find in the many boxes of stuff impeccably organized in bins in the garage. But that wasn't what made her feel so warm and fuzzy tonight.

No, that feeling was solely for what she knew she was going to find once she opened the door. She'd seen Elliot's car in the driveway, which meant he was already here waiting for her. He would've used the spare key that she kept in a plastic bag inside one of the plants that lined the side wall of the porch. Yes, she was running late again, but that had been unavoidable, as she'd had to first drop David off at the ice skating rink. Before she could leave there, she'd been stopped by Mrs. Pringle, who had more questions about the wedding and when Thomas was coming home. Hannah hadn't wanted to be rude, so there was no way she could tell Mrs. Pringle that some of her questions were a little invasive; instead, she'd dodged a lot of them in the friendliest way possible. Still, that had taken time and now she was late.

If she was totally honest, she'd been running late a lot in the past few days. Well, more like weeks. She couldn't pinpoint exactly when her schedule had begun to run over the twenty-four hours in a day, but she definitely recalled apologizing for it more often lately. Was this why Elliot wanted to get away from Evergreen? Did he think she was too busy for him and their relationship? Pausing, she sucked in a gulp of cool air, letting it out with a huff so that billows of white escaped from her lips. She wasn't too busy for Elliot. Their relationship had bloomed over the last year and had become such an integral part of her life. Besides that, she'd had a kazillion jobs before she and Elliot became a couple. He knew everything about her and he understood her like she'd thought no one else ever had. Certainly he wouldn't think this was her fault.

Deciding she was being ridiculous standing outside in the cold when a very warm house awaited her, Hannah shook her head. She rolled her neck on her shoulders and shook her arms, prepared to leave all the events of the day at the door and head inside to spend a nice quiet evening with the man she loved. Well, not so quiet—they had a gingerbread house to put together, and they'd no doubt listen to Christmas carols while doing so. That's what tonight's date was all about. Tomorrow, said gingerbread house was due at the art center where it would be on display for the morning's class. Elliot was such a dear for offering to help her with the project.

With that thought in mind, she didn't stand for another moment reminiscing about her past or addressing that niggling feeling that there might be something missing in this house she called a home. She opened the front door and stepped inside.

"Sorry I'm late," she yelled as she entered, and heard Elliot in the kitchen.

Hannah went to the closet and set the box and sheet music down on the wood floor while she removed her coat and gloves. The house was warm and she did a little shiver to get acclimated to the change in temperature. It smelled great, a combination of the bowls of pine cones she had sitting throughout the first floor and all the fresh-baked gingerbread she'd prepared before dawn this morning. Instead of leaving the box there, she picked it up with the intention of showing it to Elliot.

Walking through the narrow foyer toward the big country kitchen at the back of the house, she peeked up at familiar pictures that lined the walls. One was old, the frayed edges visible through the black frame. It was a black and white of her parents in front of the church where they'd been married. Her mother's ankle-length dress with its lace edges was still the most elegant wedding dress she'd ever seen, while her father looked debonair in his three-piece suit and fedora hat. She loved how the picture instantly brought to mind big red heart boxes of candy and jazz music, two things that were always in the house on Valentine's Day, thanks to Isaac's love for Barbara.

Another picture was of the whole family, her and Thomas seated in front of their parents, all of them sporting huge grins, happiness practically beaming through the frame. There was also contentment in those faces, as they were all happy to be together and in this town. That's the feeling that reached out to Hannah tonight, that same contentment that she'd felt all her life, even now.

"I had to drop off David at the skating pond," she said, walking into the kitchen, and immediately dropped the box and sheet music onto a counter.

"Then I ran into Mrs. Pringle and Sonya and Michelle," she continued, but paused when she noticed Elliot finishing a glass of wine.

He looked so comfortably handsome in black slacks and gray button-front shirt. When she'd seen him at the museum earlier, he'd kept his coat on so she had no idea what he'd been wearing today. His black hair had always been curly, and now he kept it longer on top and close-cut on the sides. The barest hint of a five o'clock shadow was now showing along his jaw and he looked right at home in her kitchen. The sight touched her heart. "You started without me," she said when she saw he already had the bowls filled with different candies and plates stacked with cuts of gingerbread.

"No. No," he insisted. "I had some time, so I got things ready. How were the Cooper sisters today?"

She accepted the glass of wine he offered. "You know, finishing each other's sentences and being lovely as—" Her words trailed off as she glanced into the dining room. "Elliot."

Hannah was speechless—a new thing for her—at the scene. He'd set the dining room table with white candles and sprigs of holly tucked into a red vase. There were bowls of food and two place settings on the cherry-wood table.

"Did you make dinner?" she asked.

"I did. But it's cool."

Now Hannah felt horrible. She'd been so busy taking care of everything on her schedule, then stopping to hold conversations with people she could've easily told she had plans, instead of focusing on getting here in time. She set her glass on the island and dropped her head down to groan.

In seconds, Elliot was there, touching her arm. "It's cool," he repeated.

Coming to a stand, Hannah circled the island. "Oh, it's not cool at all. I'm so sorry." She hugged him and loved how comforting it felt when he hugged her back. Her thoughts circled back to moments ago on the porch. Elliot could've been upset that she was late, yet again. He'd gone through so much to prepare dinner for her on top of his offer to help her with the gingerbread house. She should've been more considerate, should have prioritized him in the way he seemed to have done with her tonight. "I just lost track of time." It was the truth, and yet it didn't sound like enough of an excuse.

"I know," he said, pulling back a bit so he could look at her while holding her in his arms. "You're looking after your nephew; your schedule is packed with the town's Christmas needs. And you're still fitting in time to celebrate Michelle's wedding. Tell me how to help."

"This. This is what's helping. Thank you, Elliot." This was also one of the reasons she'd fallen in love with him. His ability to take any situation, examine it and figure out what he could do to make it better.

Case in point: He'd prepared dinner for her, which was a tremendous help. Otherwise she would've tossed a frozen pizza into the oven while they worked on the gingerbread house and called it a day.

"Come on, let's go sit and eat. I hope it's not too cold," she told him.

Taking her hand, he led her into the dining room. "Not in those great new ceramic dishes you bought; they really hold the heat just like you said they would."

"See, I told you they were a good investment," she said, as Elliot released her hand and pulled out a chair for her to sit.

Taking the seat as if they were at some elegant banquet dinner, she smiled up at him and watched as he moved around to the other side of the table. When he sat and then extended his hands across for her to hold, Hannah took them quickly. Elliot said a quick blessing over the food and then released her hands.

"Behold, my most famed macaroni and cheese," he said, lifting the indigo top off one of the two ceramic pots she'd purchased from the TV shopping network.

It was boxed mac 'n cheese, not homemade baked, but he always garnished it with bacon bits as his special flourish and it always made Hannah giggle because it was just the right amount of corny and romantic. "Oh, you know I love your famed mac 'n cheese."

He nodded, a goofy grin spreading across his face. "I know it."

Minutes into the meal, Elliot asked, "Hey, you remember that time the church had a spaghetti dinner and we were in charge of boiling all the noodles?"

Hannah had just set her glass of wine down and

used her napkin to wipe her mouth. "Yes, I do! We had four pots on the big stove down in the church kitchen. Two of them came from the firehouse so we could cook more at one time."

"And we put too many noodles in one of them, then lost track of time because we were so busy talking that the water started bubbling over the top," he said, forking another mouthful of mac 'n cheese into his mouth.

"Right." She was nodding now, the memory so clear in her mind. "That quickly got out of hand, and the next thing I knew you were mopping up water while I was using the strainer to catch the noodles that were coming out of the pot."

He chuckled and she did too. "I was trying to get them before they hit the floor."

"And I was trying to keep you from falling on the water, with the bowl of noodles in hand," he said after chewing and swallowing.

"Then, Mr. Finley came in asking what was going on, but we were laughing too hard to explain what had happened." Similar to the way they'd begun laughing now.

They'd had some fun times together over the years, so many that Hannah was certain they could spend every night for the next five or maybe ten years recounting them all.

"We always had a good time together," Elliot said when they quieted down a bit. "No matter what we were doing, as long as we were together, it was the best time ever."

His words were both sweet and true and Hannah couldn't help but smile. "You know, now that you say that, I realize how true it is. I mean, we've been friends for a really long time. It still amazes me that it took until last year while we were fixing the snow globe for us to realize there was something more between us."

"Well, that's how long it took you to realize it," he said. "I'd known for a while."

"Really? You never told me that." And she'd never even considered that Elliot had harbored feelings for her. Hearing this now made emotion swirl in the pit of her stomach as she slowly reached for her glass. Another sip of wine was definitely in order.

He gave that half smile that was borderline modest and heart-stopping. "I didn't know how."

After taking a sip, she set the glass down again. "What do you mean? By the time we were both in high school we were basically inseparable. I told you everything back then and I thought you were doing the same with me." Those words echoed in her mind now, because they could also relate to the fact that Elliot had been thinking about expanding the Tinker Shop but hadn't bothered to clue her in until Ezra let the plan slip.

"I was kinda nervous about telling you I wanted something more." He picked up his napkin and wiped his mouth and hands. "You know, after my parents' divorce I saw relationships in a different way. Sure, I was just a kid when they broke up, but growing up on a supposed split custody plan is a constant reminder that there was a relationship that didn't work out."

"But you barely saw your father," she said, knowing that could sometimes be a sore point for Elliot. Most often he'd acted like not going into the city to visit with his father hadn't been a problem for him, but deep down, Hannah had known it saddened him. There was a dejected look in his eyes and a slight slump to his shoulders that she'd see each time he walked up onto her front porch to say that the trip had been canceled, again. Eventually, by the time they made it to high school, that sad look had shifted to nonchalance and she figured he'd resigned himself to the circumstances and decided to just live with it. Coming from a household with two loving parents, Hannah hadn't begun to understand how he felt, so she usually just listened to him talk about his feelings whenever he felt like it. Tonight seemed like that time.

"I know, and that's what I mean. I didn't get to see a healthy relationship between two people who loved each other, so when I started feeling that way about you, I was a little skeptical about changing the dynamic of what was the closest friendship I'd ever had."

"I can see that," she said. "I had similar thoughts when I first came to the Tinker Shop with the snow globe and we were leaning in to see some of the intricate glue work and our faces were so close. We'd been close before, so many times, but that time was different." And she remembered it like it was yesterday. The quick swirl of what felt like butterflies in her stomach and that jolt of awareness that zipped through her blood.

"Yeah," he said with a nod. "Just like at the festival when we were playing that song on the piano. Or rather, I was playing and you were trying to remember the right keys."

She smiled. "You always made remembering the right keys easier." Hadn't she just been thinking about her abandoned piano lessons earlier tonight at the Cooper sisters' farm? Funny how the minute she learned that Elliot knew how to play, she'd given playing another chance.

"All those moments last year just led up to us both realizing there was more at the same time. I kind of figured it was fate."

Or that wish she'd made on the snow globe before she'd broken it. Hannah had never told Elliot about her wish. She'd never told anyone about how many times she'd actually wished on the snow globe. There was so much folklore surrounding the globe and so many happy endings tied to it that she hadn't wanted to be the only one to say she'd wished and it hadn't come true, because for so long that had been the case. She wondered how he'd react if she told him now, but decided against it. They were together now and that's all that mattered.

"Yeah," she said remembering how their love had bloomed at the most magical time of year. "It was a wish come true for me."

Reaching across the table, Elliot took her hand. "For me too, Hannah. You're the most important thing in my life; I want you to know that. I love you so much."

"Oh, Elliot, I love you too." And she did, her heart felt so full right now as she sat in the house she cherished with the man she wanted to spend the rest of her life with.

After a few moments of them simply staring into each other's eyes, Elliot finally slipped his hand from hers.

"I see a gingerbread house that still needs roofing. Come on," he said. "Let's get this table cleared and head into the kitchen."

Accepting another moment that cemented how strong and true their relationship was, Hannah followed him by taking her dishes into the kitchen and loading them with his into the dishwasher. When they were done cleaning the dining room, they both stepped up to the island in the kitchen where Elliot had set out all the supplies for the gingerbread house.

"Show me some of those Turner family gingerbread skills," he said jokingly as he popped a candy drop into his mouth.

Hannah giggled, picking up the piping bag. "Well, I never said I was an expert at this, but it'll be a presentable house when we're done."

"It'll be perfect," Elliot said looking into her eyes. "Just like you."

Warmth flooded her cheeks. Blushing had never been something she did often, but being around Elliot and filled with so much love for him was changing her in ways she'd never expected. Good ways, she thought, as they got into assembling that gingerbread house.

Chapter Eight

" Good morning!"

Elliot startled when Hannah walked up behind him. "Good morning. What're you doing here? Shouldn't you be getting ready to head over to the art center for the gingerbread contest?" Not that he didn't love seeing her; she'd been all he could think about throughout the night and as he'd prepared for his day.

It wasn't until she extended an arm toward him that he noticed she held a covered to-go cup in each hand.

"Hot cider for this chilly morning." Her smile was bright and she'd twisted her braids in the front so that they were away from her face, but left to hang long down her back. She wore faded jeans today and the deep cranberry colored coat that sometimes matched the shade of her lipstick.

Accepting the cup she offered, he couldn't help but reach out his other hand to brush a finger over her cheek. "Thanks, Hannah. You're always so thoughtful."

"Not always," she said, and looped her arm through his. "Last night got me thinking that I don't take enough time for us to just be together."

She'd started walking and Elliot fell into step with her.

"So I got up extra early this morning, ran to the Kringle to get this cider and decided to join you on your walk."

He supposed it was a good thing he walked the same path each morning. It had become a habit in the years after his mother passed away. Walking just outside the Town Square, along the streets near the house he and his mother had lived in during his teenage years, had been cathartic for him. While everyone in town had rallied around him, bringing food to his house, taking care of the flowers his mother had planted in the front yard, calling or just stopping by to say hello, Elliot had found this walk peaceful. At just after six in the morning, most of the town would be still asleep, or in their own homes tending to their morning rituals. The streets were mostly bare at this time; the quaint houses, mature trees and endless sky were normally all that met him as he strolled. And he could think freely and clearly, sort through any and all problems during this trek.

This morning, Hannah was by his side.

He lifted the cup to his lips and sipped the cider.

"You don't have to adjust your schedule for us," he said, even though a part of him recognized that his new business plan was asking her to do just that.

They hadn't talked about the Tinker Shop or her new job at the museum at all last night and he'd enjoyed the two of them just being together. So he tried to push those thoughts away this morning, opting to keep the conversation as light as possible, or to just simply follow her lead.

"I want to," she replied. "I mean, I wanted to spend some time with you before the day got started. I remember when I was little, my parents used to sit at the kitchen table and have a cup of coffee before Thomas and I got up."

He grinned. "How'd you know that's what they did if you weren't supposed to be awake?" Hannah had an innate sense of curiosity. If there was a question, she searched for an answer; something broken, she wondered how it could be fixed. He loved that about her.

"Oh, you know, I may've been an early bird even back then." She giggled. "Actually, I've always liked being up early. It's when I wrap my mind around what I have to do for the day. And anyway, the scent of the coffee brewing used to wake me up, so one morning I came downstairs, but when I heard them talking in their grown-up serious voices, I ran back upstairs. We weren't supposed to interrupt those types of conversations."

He nodded as they stepped down off a curb and walked across a tree-lined street. If they'd turned to the right, they would go down the winding road that led to the bridge. Beneath it, the ice skating rink nestled among more soaring trees now sprinkled with snow would look like a winter wonderland.

"Yeah, I remember plenty of grown-up conversations when we lived in the city."

"You never talked about that much," she said. "I

mean, about what your life was like in the city."

Because he'd never wanted his mother or anyone else to know how much he'd missed it. Thinking back on that now, he wondered if he had shared his thoughts about the city with Hannah when they were young, it would have been easier for her to understand his desire to start the new part of his life in Boston now.

He shrugged. "I thought if I talked about it I'd miss it more." The honest words slipped so easily from his lips, he couldn't believe he hadn't said them out loud before.

"What did you miss most about it?"

His immediate reply was, "The energy." When he glanced over to see her staring at him, her brows raised with interest, he continued. "Every morning after I'd have breakfast, my mother and I would take the elevator downstairs. We lived in an apartment on the tenth floor. So we'd go through the revolving doors which I played in frequently. One day I got my rain coat stuck and the doorman had to call the utility crew to get it out." The memory made him laugh. His father had been furious when he found out what happened, but Elliot had seen it as a sort of adventure.

"The moment we stepped outside the building it felt like things were alive. There were always people walking up and down the street. No matter what time. At night I could look out my bedroom window and see them. And even at seven in the morning they were out going to work, school or wherever. I hated having to hold my mother's hand while we walked to the subway. I wanted to run, dodging in and out of the people, laughing, feeling free. Of course my mother didn't let me do that, but just thinking about it every day had given me such a rush. Then there were the fast-moving subway trains and the sounds. So many sounds: car horns, people chattering, the wind on a winter's night—it was all so vibrant. I couldn't wait to get older to do all the things I hadn't been allowed to do when I was a kid."

"You wanted to be an adult running up and down the street bumping into people?" Her tone was light and laced with the humor he saw sparking in her eyes when he turned to glance at her.

"No, not exactly," he said with a grin. "I just wanted to live and feel free."

"You don't feel free here in Evergreen?"

That question was spoken seriously and Elliot took another sip of his cider to contemplate his response. This conversation wasn't turning out to be as light as he'd hoped.

"I do," he replied after they'd strolled a little further. They were on Holly Hope Drive now, just around the corner from the house where his mother used to live. In the summer the lawns were perfectly maintained rows of green, driveways either filled with parked cars or children playing with their toys. Now, the grass was covered with a couple inches of snow, the shrubs around the house wrapped with twinkle lights.

"Evergreen was so different than where I'd come from," he admitted. "My mother loved the peaceful-ness here, the sound of the birds chirping on summer mornings and the look of the snow covering everything in the winter." He glanced to his right at a house they were passing.

It was a white Cape Cod style home with dark green shutters at every window. The Zalinskis lived there with Moxy and Iris, the two greyhounds they'd adopted from the Greystone Network. As if on command from his thoughts, the front door opened and Mr. Zalinski came out with the dogs on their leashes.

"Mornin', Elliot! And hey, Hannah, he's got you out early this morning too," Mr. Zalinski said, waving at the two of them as the dogs pulled in front of him, eager to get down the front steps.

"Good morning, Mr. Zalinski," Elliot said, lifting the hand that held his cup of cider.

"Good morning," Hannah chimed from beside him. "Hi, Moxy and Iris!"

The dogs responded by wagging their tails, Iris grinning in Hannah's direction.

Mr. Zalinski came down to the end of the walkway where Elliot and Hannah had stopped. Hannah immediately leaned in to pet Iris and then a not-to-be-ignored Moxy.

"Pretty soon you'll be walking your own dogs along these streets, or possibly pushing a baby stroller." Mr. Zalinksi wiggled his busy gray eyebrows and Elliot's brow furrowed.

"I like dogs," Hannah said, not noticing Elliot's reaction. "My father was allergic so we couldn't have one. But I'd love to own one someday."

Elliot hadn't known that, and he continued to stare at the dogs. They were cute—Moxy with his shiny gray coat, and Iris with her gorgeous black-and-white coloring—but he'd never dreamed of having a dog when he was little. There were no pets allowed in the apartment building where they'd lived in the city.

Certainly he could find an apartment building in Boston that allowed pets. And if not, perhaps a townhouse with a lawn and backyard. Wouldn't that be similar enough to Holly Hope Drive?

"They're good pals," Mr. Zalinski was saying when Elliot forced himself to pay attention to the here and now. "And most of them are great with kids."

On a normal morning, Elliot would've waved at Mr. Zalinksi and the dogs and kept on walking. Why they were standing here having a conversation that for some reason kept circling back to children, he had no idea.

"So I've heard," Hannah replied, when the dogs had finally lost interest in her petting them.

Now they were tugging on their leashes again and Mr. Zalinksi chuckled. "Well, gotta go. These two are ready to get a move on."

"Have a great day," Elliot said with another wave.

"Yeah, you too, Iris and Moxy," Hannah yelled with a chuckle and wave to the dogs.

She really did like them. He shook his head as they continued to walk. "They've got a lot of energy," he said, watching the dogs pull Mr. Zalinski across the street, where he unleashed them and let them run through the wide-open area on that side.

"The same kind of energy you wanted to find in the city," Hannah replied.

They continued walking and the conversation shifted to what they had planned for today—Hannah had the gingerbread contest at the art center and he had to get to the Tinker Shop to open up for the woodwork class. Then they were meeting up again at Henry's farm to pick up the trees Hannah ordered for the museum. The subject of him living in the city didn't come up again and Elliot couldn't figure out if he were happy or sad about that.

On the one hand, he realized the discussion could've been a great preface to the talk they needed to have about his new business venture. On the other, he hadn't missed the way Hannah's inquisitive tone when she'd asked about his life in the city had quickly changed to exuberant happiness with the appearance of Moxy and Iris and her admission that she'd always wanted a dog. Not to mention the children—although Hannah hadn't been the one to bring them up. After he'd headed to the Tinker Shop and Hannah had returned home to pick up the gingerbread house, he'd thought about that part a little more. Children, dogs, walks along streets that looked and felt like Holly Hope Drive—Elliot didn't know if he could compete with that. He didn't know if asking Hannah to leave all she knew, loved and hoped for was even fair at this point. All he knew for certain was that he loved her and he wanted to be with her.

He also wanted to open the second shop in Boston and to see how his life would be if he did the things he'd always hoped for.

"Thanks for saving us the best trees," Elliot said to Henry later that morning when they were at the Christmas tree farm.

They were standing at the red truck now, Elliot loading the trees into the back while Henry supervised his staff to bring them the appropriate ones.

"And for all your help—really, it's amazing, Henry." Hannah was more than grateful to Henry for all he'd been doing at the Tinker Shop, and now for the trees that he was donating to the Christmas Museum.

"Awww, no thanks necessary. I'm just excited for the museum opening. It's the talk of the town. Besides, with Kevin and Lisa up north this year, I'm spending Christmas alone. So helping out around town keeps me busy," he replied.

Over Henry's shoulder, Hannah had seen Michelle's car pull up. She and Sonya were just walking up to meet Hannah and Henry where they stood. Sonya grabbed her coat and pulled it close against the bitter chill of the day.

"Come on now, Henry. You know that no one in the history of Evergreen has ever spent Christmas alone," Michelle told him when she stood a few feet from the truck.

"She's right," Hannah added, coming over to give Henry a quick hug. "You have us."

"Henry, this is my sister Sonya." Michelle introduced

them and Henry took a step to stand in front of Sonya.

"Merry Christmas," Henry said, staring at Sonya with an intrigued smile on his face.

"Nice to meet you," Sonya replied, returning his direct gaze.

If Hannah hadn't know better, she would've thought there was some type of spark between these two.

"Oh, Michelle," Henry said when he was finally able to stop staring at Sonya. "The barn is all ready for the rehearsal dinner."

"This is that barn?" Sonya asked, looking over Henry's shoulder. "It's bigger than I thought it'd be."

There was a brisk breeze blowing today and it ruffled Michelle's hair. She tucked it back behind her ear and replied, "Thank you so much for letting us have our rehearsal dinner here. Thomas loves coming out here so he's gonna be thrilled."

"When does he get back?" Henry asked.

"Well, there's a snowstorm in Maine and he called last night to say they're having a little bit of trouble closing down the logging camp." She hesitated and then shook her head. "But everything's gonna be fine."

Hannah and Sonya exchanged a worried look, but both avoided sharing that look with Michelle.

"Yep," Hannah said. "So now that we have one last tree for the museum, we'll get it decorated and hang up the rest of those pictures."

"Do you need my help?" Michelle asked hopefully.

"Nah, like I told you before, you just enjoy getting ready for your wedding," Hannah replied. "Right now, we need to get going. We've got a busy day ahead."

Michelle and Henry both chuckled. "You've always got a busy day ahead, Hannah," Michelle said.

Hannah grinned and waved at them. Elliot closed the back of the truck and tossed her the keys. Catching them, Hannah made her way around to the driver's side of the truck and got inside.

"You always get that ribbon just right," Elliot told Hannah later that morning when they were at the Christmas Museum.

"Yeah," she replied, "but you have a great eye for balancing the ratio of ornaments with bulbs. I always just put them all up and hope for the best."

They were decorating one of the trees they'd just picked up from Henry's farm. This one was the biggest balsam fir, the one that Henry had suggested for the entrance because its strong branches would hold the most decorations. In the other rooms they had a mixture of Douglas and Fraser firs that were just as beautiful and smelled absolutely perfect.

"Well, the best is always what happens once you're finished. This red and white color scheme is festive and elegant," he continued.

"Yeah, I love this plaid ribbon with the tiny specks of silver throughout. I think we should order more of this for the Tinker Shop."

"Okay, I'll put that on our supply list for the next order. Oh, and those clear bulbs. We've been going through those in the ornament-making class."

"Right," she said, enjoying the easy companionship as much as decorating the tree.

When they were done, Hannah climbed up on the ladder to put a delicate filigree star on top.

"There," Elliot said, helping her down off the ladder. "Nice work."

"We made the entrance look better already," she replied, and folded her arms over her chest. A quick glance over at Elliot and she saw that he was standing the same way. "Now, to get old Uncle Scrooge down and hung in another room."

Elliot walked over to the wall where the picture of Hiram Cooper hung. "Well, out with the old," he said as he took down the oval-shaped antique frame.

"Hmmm," she said tilting her head. "What do you think should go over there?"

"Hmmm, maybe something like—" His words trailed off as he moved away from her to dig into one of the boxes sitting on the floor. "This," he said, and returned to stand beside her. He showed her the picture he'd taken out of the box.

Hannah leaned in close so she could see it and beamed as she recognized the old photo.

"Oh, wow, it's the mural my parents painted in Kringle Alley." She held one side of the picture while Elliot held the other. Her parents stood proudly in front of the mural, their hands joined, smiles on their faces. Her chest tightened. "It's a shame it was taken down."

"Well, what if we recreated it?"

Tears instantly stung her eyes as a mixture of reminiscing about her parents and Elliot's sweet offer collided.

"Yeah," she said with a nod, trying to keep the quick flush of emotion from overtaking her. "That would be a nice way to honor them."

"I'll get started figuring it out when I get to the Tinker Shop," he said.

"Okay." She took a deep steadying breath and reached for his hand. "And thanks for letting me join you on your walk and helping me with the trees today."

With a smile Elliot took her other hand, and leaned in closer to kiss her gently on the lips. He pulled back only slightly but they continued to stare at each other. In those few moments there was nothing else, no place to rush off to, no job to complete, just her and Elliot, and Hannah loved it.

"You're most welcome, Hannah Turner," Elliot whispered.

After another quick kiss he was gone, and Hannah was in the entryway alone once again, her thoughts returning to what else she could add to the space. When she heard the front door open and close, she just assumed Elliot had forgotten something and come back for it. The unfamiliar brusque voice shocked her.

"What are you doing with that?"

Hannah laughed and turned around to see the visitor walking in. "Oh, goodness. You scared me."

The man wearing a surly expression and a long black coat walked farther into the entrance, looking around as if he'd lost something. Hannah was too busy trying to figure out who he was and what he wanted to notice anything else about him at the moment.

"Hi. Um, can I help you…?" Hannah said, and when he just kept walking she continued, "Can I help you with something?"

He strode farther into the space, going close to another box, and picked up an ornament, then dropped it back down into the box.

"What do you think you're doing, exactly?"

"In life?" Hannah asked, only half-jokingly.

"What are you doing with the old Hat Factory?" He came closer to her.

Now she got a better look at him. His hair, from what she could see from beneath his smoke-gray fedora, was salt and pepper gray, his eyes a cooler shade of the same gray tone. Thin lips were drawn tightly and his brow was furrowed, confirming her first impression that he was surly for some reason. Try as she might, though, she didn't recognize him. Evergreen was a very friendly town and Hannah knew just about everyone who lived there. But Christmas was a big tourist season, so she assumed this guy was one of them. Not one that she needed to be afraid of, she presumed, but still. "Well, um, hi. I'm Hannah. I'm the new manager of the Evergreen Christmas Museum. And who might you be?"

He'd walked past her again, seeming to ignore her question for a second time.

"I'm looking for Jenny and Josie Cooper," he said with a passing glance over his shoulder.

Still baffled by this whole exchange and now actually wishing the unfriendly man would just leave, Hannah shrugged. "Well, I haven't seen them. Have you tried the farm?"

His response was a heavy sigh before he turned and walked out the door, leaving Hannah alone once again, and very confused.

"Merry Christmas," she said with a wave to his retreating back.

Chapter Nine

*E*lliot and Ezra walked through the Town Square after having a nice lunch at the Kringle. They'd both gotten a peppermint mocha eggnog to go from David, and were now holding the insulated travel cups in their gloved hands, steam rising from the tops.

"And don't get me wrong, I love Evergreen," Ezra said. "But in Boston, I can be anyone. Sure, I've made friends, but sometimes when I just want some time alone, without being Ezra Green, former mayor, son of Evergreen—"

Janie Crown came out of the dress shop just as they were walking by.

"Hi, Ezra!" Janie said with a quick wave. "Hey, Elliot."

"Hey, Janie. It's good to see you," Ezra replied, easily slipping back into the role of town mayor who knew everybody. "How's your mom?"

"Oh, she's doing just fine," Janie replied.

"Tell her I asked about her," Ezra continued. "And have a Merry Christmas!"

"I will, and Merry Christmas to you too!" Janie waved as she walked across the street heading to Daisy's.

"You see what I mean," Ezra said, the moment she was out of earshot.

Elliot grinned. "Yeah, I do. I'm happy for you, man. I have to admit, while part of me hopes I get this money, another part of me doesn't want things to change." Especially everything he'd finally found with Hannah. After his walk this morning he'd been thinking a lot about what he loved most about being in this town. Of course that was Hannah, but second to that was the way everybody knew everybody and made the effort to be friendly. Mr. Zalinksi and the greyhounds had been a great reminder.

"That's the thing about the future. We don't know what change looks like until we get there. But you have to let change happen to you."

Elliot heard Ezra's words and could totally understand them on some level. "I don't know," he said. "I mean, things between me and Hannah are so great right now." Well, that was partially true. He had been wishing they'd have more time together in the past few months and now, apparently Hannah was thinking along those lines too. "I don't want to mess that up."

"I understand. I thought moving to Boston was going to make things better between Oliver and me, but we just couldn't seem to find our groove once I got there." Ezra took a sip from his cup.

"Relationships take work," Elliot said, as if he were now a relationship guru. That couldn't be further from the truth. Like he'd told Hannah last night, he'd been so hung up on the failure of his parents' relationship that he'd wasted so many years not telling Hannah how he really felt about her.

He actually didn't know what he was doing as far as being in a relationship. All he knew for certain was that he didn't want to end up like his parents. With one person hating the other for not being what they expected.

"I hear ya," Ezra replied. "But listen, you and Hannah have a great thing going with the business too. You told me yourself how easy it's been making all these new additions to the Tinker Shop together. I'm sure that chemistry would just carry over to Boston. And you'd love the city."

They crossed the street, Ezra waving to someone else he knew and Elliot watching as the Christmas Festival sign was hung along the entrance to the area where it would be held this year.

"I don't doubt that we'd work well together wherever we are," Elliot said. "I'm just a little concerned about all that Hannah has going on here. I mean, can I really ask her to leave all this?" He looked around at the holiday decorations and listened to the Christmas carols playing through the loud speakers. "She grew up here; this town is all she knows."

"All the more reason to want a new adventure." Ezra tapped his arm. "Look, I've lived here all my life too, but believe me when I tell you it was refreshing to be somewhere else, doing something different. Something that was just about *me*, Ezra, not the son of the former mayor who'd eventually become mayor himself."

Elliot nodded. "Yeah, I'd love for Hannah to see more of the world and to really get the chance to grow in a new place. We could be a totally different couple in Boston. Doing new and fun things."

They could do those things together: build another chapter of their life with a new business opportunity in a place they could call their own. It was what Elliot had been dreaming of this past year and what he hoped with all his heart was possible.

"It's really coming down out there," Thomas said via another FaceTime call with Michelle.

She was sitting in her family room while Sonya was in a chair across from her attempting to wrap some presents. But her mind was totally focused on the face on her phone's screen. In addition to being charming, compassionate and a great father, Thomas was a very handsome man. It hit her at that moment how much she'd missed seeing his face with its root beer-brown complexion, the close cut of his beard and his bald head in person.

"So you think you'll be back...wait, do you think you're gonna get held up?" It was what Michelle had been afraid of all day, but now with Thomas's words the fear was becoming all the more real. Her stomach twisted as dread settled in.

He frowned. "I mean, it's hard to say right now."

"So there is a chance you won't make it back in time." Michelle couldn't believe this was happening after all the planning she'd done. It was all she could do to remain calm. When there was now a pounding in her chest and her breaths were coming just a little faster. She tried to think of something positive to ward off the growing panic. With so many thoughts running through her mind at this moment, focusing on the good wasn't easy. And trying to keep this conversation going without making Thomas feel worse about a weather event that neither of them could control was an even bigger task.

"Well, no." He paused. "Maybe."

Oh no, that wasn't good. She sighed, on the verge of totally losing it. "Thomas, if you're stuck in Maine for our wedding…"

"Michelle Lansing," he said, "if I have to move mountains of snow with my bare hands, I will be there."

She let out a shaky breath and closed her eyes briefly. While she loved hearing the determination in his voice, she definitely didn't want anything to happen to him, or anyone else. "Well, you may want that, but we can't predict the weather and safety's first. I love you," she said, because panic and hurt that she didn't want him to witness threatened her next words.

"I love you, too. Oh, don't forget what I said. Don't be afraid to ask your sister about your dad. She's got your back."

With that, Michelle looked over to where Sonya had been sitting in the light blue armchair pretending not to be eavesdropping and fiddling with the bow on a gift.

"Okay, all right," Michelle said a little louder now, praying Sonya hadn't heard him. "I gotta go." She blew him a kiss before disconnecting the call and tossing a wary look to her sister.

"Oh boy, here we go," Sonya said, putting the box she'd been holding down and rubbing her hands along her thighs.

So that prayer had been futile and Michelle knew there was no way around having this conversation. Perhaps she could use her frustration about the wedding and worry over Thomas's safety as an excuse. The last thing she wanted to do right now was have this discussion with Sonya, but she knew there was no way around it now.

With a huff Michelle shook her head. "Well, every single time I ask Dad what day he's arriving, he gives me some new excuse. Now he's closing up his house for some potential storm. I know the man hates travel in winter for fear of getting stuck somewhere, but come on."

Her father didn't often leave their hometown of North Carolina, and when he did, it was almost always in the summer months when he knew nothing like the weather catastrophe that Thomas was facing could keep him from returning. The house he'd bought for his wife and daughters was Gordon's pride and joy.

Michelle looked around at her own oasis, loving the sky-blue, silver and white decorations she'd scattered throughout. Even now, sitting in the family room that opened up to the kitchen on one side and the formal living room on the other, she tried to extract the desperately needed calm from her surroundings.

"You know how he is," Sonya continued. "Sometimes when he doesn't know what to do, he avoids checking in." Sonya stood and came over to sit on the couch beside Michelle.

Michelle watched her pick up a roll of wrapping paper and look at one of the other unwrapped boxes. "Well, that means something's wrong," she said.

When Sonya didn't respond, but instead looked away, Michelle picked up another roll of wrapping paper and smacked her playfully on the leg with it. Sonya grabbed a roll of wrapping paper and took a swing at Michelle. They jumped up and started a wrapping paper sword fight. Michelle felt like they were back in their teenage years.

"We're doing this," Sonya said. "Again." Her tone was both exasperated and incredulous, but the way she was readily engaging, a light of excitement in her eyes, almost had Michelle smiling.

"Remember when we were young and we used to make cards for mom and dad and somehow glitter would just end up all in my hair? Nobody could figure out why." Of course, that was the memory that popped into her head. It always did whenever Michelle thought of Christmas with her sister, because it was one of the fondest times in her life. Her family had been together then, her mother alive and well, all of them celebrating the holiday together as they always had. It was an amazing time.

"I already apologized for that," Sonya said through clenched teeth, and got in another whack against Michelle's wrapping paper sword.

Michelle leaned forward and reached for the container of glitter that had been left out after she'd dipped bulbs yesterday.

"Oh no, not glitter," Sonya said, backing away. "Glitter never goes away."

Michelle followed her sister with the container of glitter extended toward her in a taunt. Sonya skirted around the couch to get away, but Michelle followed her.

"Okay. Okay," Sonya said, stopping and holding out a hand in truce. "Dad and I may or may not have had a small falling out."

Michelle stopped, her whole demeanor shifting to concern. "About what?"

When Sonya hesitated, Michelle extended her hand with the glitter again, pushing it right up in Sonya's face, as if all she had to do was flip off the cap and douse her with the blue and silver sprinkles.

"He asked me not to talk about it until he can explain in person," Sonya blurted out.

Michelle immediately paused. "Is that good or bad?"

Sonya shrugged. "It is what it is," she said, and got in one last swing with the wrapping paper sword before dropping it and running out to the kitchen.

Left alone now, Michelle didn't know what to think. Just like she didn't know what was going to happen with Thomas and that snowstorm. Trying not to have one of her infamous panic attacks, Michelle focused on steadying her breathing. Telling herself that all was going to be well. Her father was going to arrive, and she'd have her family here. Then Thomas would make it home, and they'd have the gorgeous wedding they'd planned.

That's how things were going to turn out; they had to. Or she was definitely going to have a complete meltdown.

Later that evening as another busy day was winding down for Hannah and she was just about to wrap things up at the Inn and head home, another surprise visitor appeared.

"You seem to be everywhere."

Hannah looked up from where she stood at the front desk, sealing the last of the Christmas card envelopes, to see the grumpy man who'd come into the Christmas Museum this afternoon. He was standing there with the same scowl he'd had earlier, and she still didn't know why.

"Yep," she said in an even tone. "That's me, Hannah Turner." And then finding her Evergreen spirit, she smiled and spoke cordially. "I never caught your name earlier."

"Jeb Cooper," he said, and walked toward the front desk. "Brother of Josie and Jenny Cooper."

"Oh." She nodded, wondering why she'd never seen, or heard of, Josie and Jenny's brother before now.

"My sisters had no right to hand you the keys to that factory." He punctuated his words by pointing the hand holding his hat toward her. His entire demeanor was a mixture of sad and disgruntled and Hannah wondered if he'd always been this way.

"I should've been consulted," he continued. "Especially before you moved the portrait of the factory founder, Hiram Cooper."

"Well, I wasn't aware that...that... I mean, I'm sure we can come to some sort of agreement," she said, finding yet another smile to offer the man who truly seemed to want no part of being happy.

"I'm sure you'll find you're wrong," he said solemnly, and walked away.

He had a penchant for doing that. Regardless of the fact that it was rude and dismissive. With a frown, Hannah tried to dismiss him, but she had a sinking suspicion that she hadn't seen the last of Jeb Cooper.

Chapter Ten

The next day after a call from the Cooper sisters, Hannah's presumption that she'd see Jeb Cooper again came to fruition.

She and Elliot stood in the Cooper sisters' living room, while the sisters sat at a table assembling a tiny Christmas village. On any other day, being there would've been enjoyable; Josie and Jenny were always a hoot to be around. And their house was nothing short of a fabulous rendition of small town living with a huge dose of Evergreen's Christmas spirit thrown in. They had more decorations around the place than even Hannah could've imagined. And the best part was that most of their stuff was homemade. Josie and Jenny had always been excellent crafters, and often helped out at the art center or for whatever other event the town had going on.

Today's visit, however, wasn't a friendly one. Hannah struggled to keep her festive demeanor.

"My sisters never consulted me about whether or not the town could use the building," Jeb told Hannah as they both stood in the middle of the living room.

"Now, Jeb," the sisters said simultaneously.

"You haven't taken an interest in that building in the last thirty years. Nor have you bothered to set foot in Evergreen during that time," Jenny said. "Elliot, uh, hand me the little post office, will you?"

Elliot, who'd been standing next to Hannah, quickly moved to get the piece from the many boxes on the other side of the room. "Uh, sure. Just let me see if I can find it," he replied.

"We naturally assumed you wouldn't mind," Josie said, returning to the Hat Factory conversation. Josie wore a red turtleneck today—which coincidentally would've matched her sister's glasses perfectly—and Jenny wore a blue one.

When Elliot found the post office, he took it to Jenny. Josie touched his arm before he could move away. "Oh, and can you get that little ice skating piece?"

Hannah watched Elliot nod and return to the box across the room. Jeb continued on, "Well, you assumed wrong. I was the last person to run the Hat Factory business, so shouldn't I have some say in what happens to the building?"

"And we're happy to work with you," Hannah spoke up. She'd been listening to Jeb's arguments since arriving there twenty minutes ago; the man just didn't seem to be hearing her.

"Which is why I've set up a call with the town council," Jeb said. "The legacy of the Hat Factory should not be reduced to some quaint little tourist attraction."

When Jeb walked away this time, Hannah called after him to no avail.

She finally turned to ask the sisters, "Does he always do that?"

"He's been a moody one all his life," Josie said. "Mother used to say to give him space and he'd come around."

Jenny shook her head. "He rarely ever did," she said.

"It'll be fine," Elliot said, coming over to take Hannah's hand. "I'm sure the town council will handle the situation and the museum will open as planned."

Hannah took a deep breath, exhaled it slowly and tried to focus on his comforting words. "I hope so. I have so many great plans for the museum and I know that the people of the town are gonna love it. Besides that, we're already expecting reporters and photographers to show up and write stories that'll garner more publicity for the museum. Michelle already had this huge promotional push all worked out to kick off at the first of the year. We're hoping to get tourists all year long with this new attraction, not just the seasonal ones."

"Take another breath," Elliot said, this time placing his hands on Hannah's shoulders.

"She should sit down and put her head between her knees if she's hyperventilating," Jenny said over her shoulder.

"She's not hyperventilating," Elliot replied, while Hannah looked quizzically at the Cooper sister who'd already turned back to her Christmas town project. "She just needs to slow down and let somebody else handle this."

"But I'm the manager of the museum," Hannah replied, returning her gaze to Elliot. "It's my job to make sure everything goes smoothly."

"It's the town council's job to secure the building legally," he told her. "Let them handle Jeb Cooper while you continue on with your other responsibilities."

Hannah knew Elliot was right. There was nothing else she could do where the very stubborn Jeb Cooper was concerned. He'd already decided not to like her or anything that came out of her mouth, and she wasn't going to change that fact. At least not today, anyway.

"You're right," she told him. "Let's get back to the Tinker Shop. I've got more mugs and mittens to take over to Daisy's."

Elliot nodded. "That sounds like a plan."

Jeb Cooper was going to be a problem. Of that, Elliot was sure, but it was his job to keep Hannah from worrying about that problem too much. Suggesting she let the town council handle Jeb and his complaints from this point on was only the start. He planned to continue helping her out with the other things she was taking care of so she wouldn't become stressed. Now, if he could also make her see that asking for and accepting help wasn't a bad thing, he'd be on a roll.

As it stood, as they walked out of the Cooper sisters' house together, he would simply accept that she was letting him help her make deliveries today.

"Oh, hey, you two." Carol spoke cheerfully. She was coming up the walkway just as Elliot and Hannah walked down the steps. "Nice bumping into you."

"Hey, Carol," Elliot replied when he and Hannah came to a stop.

"Hi!" Hannah said, putting on her mittens. "We were just talking to the Cooper twins about the museum. What're you doing here?"

"Well, I just wanted to make sure that the twins got one of the first printings. Ta-dah!" She turned the book in her arms around so they could see the title. "The Kris Kringle Kitchen Cookbook" had a festive green cover and a picture of a jolly Santa in the center.

"It's an early Christmas gift," Carol continued with a proud grin.

"That's amazing!" Elliot said. "Congratulations."

He couldn't have been happier for Carol. She and Joe were great people who'd reached out to offer his mother help more than once. Elliot also loved eating at the Kringle Kitchen, just as most of the people of the town did. It was wonderful to see her sharing those recipes with the world.

"Hopefully we'll be selling them at the shop soon, too," he continued.

"Oh, yes. That's right. Having them at the Tinker Shop would be fabulous," Hannah said.

"Oh, I'd love that," Carol told them. "Thanks. Now, I need to get inside. It's cold out here. You guys have a great day."

"Well, they were working on the Christmas town

when we left, so be prepared to help find some pieces once you get inside," Elliot said when she passed him.

"Oh boy! I love Christmas towns," Carol said, and started up the steps.

Hannah was already ahead of Elliot when he looked around to see the fresh snow that had fallen sometime after he'd gone to sleep last night. There were about six or seven inches on the Cooper sisters' front lawn and the air was a fresh brisk breeze. A memory sparked in his mind and he caught up with Hannah, reaching out to touch her elbow.

"Hey," he said and she turned to him.

"What?"

"This is where we met." Dropping his hand from her, he used the other arm to extend to the space around them. The memory was so clear in his mind, he could almost see their pre-teen selves right here all those years ago.

Hannah followed his gaze, staring for just a few seconds before smiling back at him. "Oh yeah."

"You had piano lessons. That you were taking reluctantly," Hannah said.

"Yeah. And you were…always here. Even after you stopped your piano lessons."

"I always loved coming here after school, even if the lessons weren't a good fit for me. And my parents were fine with the Cooper sisters looking after me for a couple hours."

"Sometimes, because I usually got here before you did, I'd look out the window and see when you arrived.

If there was snow out, you always stopped to play in it before coming inside." He touched a finger to her cheek, enjoying the way she leaned in to the touch.

"Oh wow, you spied on me?"

She was adorable when she blushed. "I wouldn't say spied. Admired you from afar sounds much better."

"We were so young then."

"I always noticed you, Hannah." And he knew he'd never stop. She was an unforgettable part of his life who meant more to him than anything else in the world.

"Actually," he said, taking her hand and walking them forward. "You were right here making snow angels."

She laughed. "I still like making snow angels. And then you threw a snowball at me."

"Yeah, and then you taught me how to make a better snowball."

"Well, yeah. Because you'd come from the city and there's a difference between their snowballs and an Evergreen snowball."

He nodded with a grin. "You said the most important part was you can't let it stick to your mittens."

"It is," she said arms wide, grinning with the memory. "It really is. Well, we should probably get to the Tinker Shop." She turned to go.

Not ready to let the memory end and get back to the busy schedules of the day, Elliot didn't follow her, but instead knelt down to pack a handful of snow. In the next seconds he aimed and released, watching as the snowball smacked into her back.

"Hey!" she yelled and turned back to him.

For just a second, he thought she was going to tell him they didn't have time for this, and Elliot held his breath with impending disappointment. But then, her lips spread into a smile and she said, "Oh, it's on now."

She bent down to pack her own snowball and he knew he had to hurry into action. Hannah was good at a lot of things, but she was great at snowball fights.

He didn't know how many snowballs they tossed at each other, how many she landed with perfect precision in the center of his back, on his shoulder, or once even to the back of his head so the cold wet snow slithered down into his jacket. Or how long they'd played around out there, but he didn't care. All Elliot knew was that these were the whimsical fun times he missed with Hannah. Moments like this when nothing seemed to exist but the two of them were what he wanted to capture and hold on to forever.

So when she threw another snowball and then began to run away, he reached out, caught her around the waist with his arm and brought her back to him. The effort was so quick, and since she'd been in flight when it happened, he lost his footing and they both fell onto the snow. Laughing like happy kids, he kept his arms around her as they rolled over in the snow, loving the feel of her so close to him, not only in proximity, but also in spirit.

When he finally let go of her so they both could breathe, Hannah fell onto her back and he did the same. Only seconds passed before they turned to stare at each other. It was an unspoken decision, but then they both spread out their arms and legs and began moving them in the snow.

"What's better than snowball fights?" she asked, the way she had so many years ago in this very spot.

"Snow angels." When he looked over at her, he could've sworn he was staring at the most perfect snow angel ever born.

"Oh, those two are so sweet," Carol said as she stood at the window in the Cooper sisters' music room.

When she'd knocked on the door, Josie had come to open it and Jenny had gotten up from the table where they were assembling the Christmas town. It had only taken a few minutes for talk about the cookbook to lead to the Kringle and that led to talk of the upcoming festival. The festival discussion brought up the topic of the choir and what music they were singing this year. But Carol had moved to the large window the moment they arrived in the music room. It had always drawn her here when she was younger and she couldn't resist now.

"Who are you referring to, dear?" Josie asked.

"Hannah and Elliot. They're out front playing in the snow. I love how they finally found each other and now are able to enjoy every aspect of their lives together."

"True love," the Cooper sisters said in unison.

Carol didn't have to turn from the window to know that the sisters were standing close together. They usually were whenever they spoke as one.

"I remember Hannah growing up with Allie. The

two of them being in the same class. Barbara and I watching them play in the park or down by the skating pond together. They've remained so close all these years. But when Allie moved to Paris with Ryan, Hannah was kind of just here filling up all her time with one task after another," Carol said, watching as Hannah and Elliot began making snow angels. There was a genuine smile on Hannah's face, one that Carol knew would've filled Barbara with happiness to see.

"Well, she and Michelle are going to be sisters now," Josie said. "And everyone in town loves Hannah."

"Yeah." Carol agreed with a nod. "And we love Elliot too. He's so perfect for her."

"Yes, he is," Jenny added.

"I hope she can finally slow down and enjoy all the happiness that was meant for her," Carol continued, pondering her conversation with Hannah at the church a couple days ago. Then, as if remembering where she was and why she was here, she turned to face the Cooper sisters and said, "Anyway, thanks for letting me come up and look at this room. It's been so long since I've been in here."

She walked across the room, passing the cello and harp that were set up in the center and going over to the corner where the piano had always sat. Rubbing her hand over the top of the piano where the sisters had placed a long white lace runner and a sleigh-shaped centerpiece filled with pinecones and colorful Christmas bulbs, she continued to look around. The walls were painted a soft ivory, the mantel above the fireplace on one side was flanked by garlands filled with bright holly berries. Wide clear jars with white candles inside were lit, and a beautiful tree decorated in gold, green and red with lots of gold ribbon sat near another window.

"Well, thank you for gifting us the first copy of your recipe book. It's so kind," Jenny replied.

"Earlier I was thinking about the piano lessons I'd take with you two," Carol said as she continued to run her hand along the piano. "I think you've taught just about everyone in town how to play one instrument or another."

"You were such a good student," Jenny told her with a warm smile.

"And don't forget those many years you were in our bell choir," Josie added with a nod.

"Oh, I totally forgot about the handbell choir," Carol exclaimed.

With Jenny by her side, as always, Josie leaned over and slid back the doors of what looked like an antique cabinet with its scratched dark wood surface, to reveal a set of handbells.

Carol gasped. "Oh, you're kidding me." She leaned down so she could see them closer. "We used to play all kinds of Christmas concerts on these." Reaching forward she took one out, then stood to shake it.

The sound rang throughout the room in one rhythmic chime and the Cooper sisters sighed with delight. Carol stared at the bell, memories flooding her senses.

"The handbell collection goes way back in our family. All the way back to Hiram Cooper," Jenny said.

Josie tapped a finger to her chin before adding to the story. "Our mom and dad loved the sound of these. But bell choirs fell out of fashion right about the time you were a teenager."

"More people wanted to sing rather than play the bells, so we formed the choir, and put them in here," Jenny continued. "You're welcome to come by and play anytime."

"Oh," Carol said, still holding the bell in her hand. "I'd love to. The sound of the bells, especially during Christmas, brings such a warm nostalgic feeling."

With a sorrowful shake of her head, Josie replied, "I don't think this generation will agree."

"I don't know," Carol said, an idea already forming in her mind. "There's always a way to make the old new again."

Chapter Eleven

"This has been such a great day," Hannah said as she and Elliot walked toward the Inn. "First, the snowballs and snow angels, then some work at the Tinker Shop and then a long lunch at the Kringle." She rubbed her stomach. "Those eggnog waffles were delicious, especially when I added the country fried chicken strips."

"Yeah," Elliot replied, holding her hand tightly as they continued. "Carol loved that idea, said she was going to talk to Joe about adding the combo to the menu."

"As well she should. The maple syrup from the Sugar Shack is amazing on both. I'm so full now I could lie down and take a long nap." She moaned at the thought.

"When's the last time you did that?" he asked. "Took a long afternoon nap?"

She considered that question for a moment, scrunching her face with the effort. "Not since I was a little girl, I think."

"My mother used to say a nap, even as short as

fifteen minutes—a cat nap, she used to call it—could do a world of good."

"I don't think there's fifteen minutes in my schedule to even consider such a delight. As it is, I spent most of our lunch going over ideas for the museum with you and talking about all the things from the Tinker Shop we're going to stock in the gift shop." She shrugged. "That didn't even count as just a lovely lunch with my boyfriend."

Saying that aloud made her feel some type of way. She couldn't quite put her finger on what the feeling was, but she knew she didn't like it.

"Yeah, but at least we were together. I like spending time with you, Hannah. It reminds me of the old days, especially during the summer when we spent all our time together."

They had done that, Hannah recalled. Especially those last two years she was in high school. Whatever job she was doing or activity she participated in, Elliot was never far behind. Thinking back now, that could be because he'd had a crush on her, or so he'd told her the other night, but Hannah had always just thought it was nice to have her best friend so close by.

"I want you to promise me something," Elliot said as they came closer to the steps that would lead to Meg's front porch.

"What's that?"

"Promise me that after Christmas you'll think about taking a little break. Maybe a trip or something, just to get away from Evergreen and take a breath from all your responsibilities here."

Instinct had her thinking of exactly that: all the responsibilities she had in town. The museum would be newly open and surely she'd be needed there. Michelle and Thomas would be away on their honeymoon, so if David was still in town, she'd have to keep an eye on him. Meg might have a lull in business the first and second week in January, but Valentine's Day was just around the corner, and Evergreen did a huge celebration for that holiday as well.

"On one condition." She smiled as she heard herself say it.

"And that's?"

"That you go with me. We could make it a couple's vacation, because you've been working really hard at the Tinker Shop, too."

When he leaned in to kiss the tip of her nose and replied, "You got it," Hannah warmed all over. Pulling Elliot into a hug, she closed her eyes to the image of them being like this forever. Living and working in Evergreen, eventually having a family of their own. It all seemed so close to reality now, so easy to imagine, that she was bursting with excitement by the time they walked into the Inn.

Everyone was already in the kitchen working on baking the hundreds of cookies they were gonna need for the festival. She and Elliot removed their coats and headed back, jumping in to help.

Sonya poured a bag of chocolate chips into a glass bowl. She popped one into her mouth and marveled as she chewed. "You do this every year?" she asked nobody in particular, since the kitchen was full of people happily moving around.

David was standing closest to her at the massive center island, scooping out already-made chocolate chip cookie dough and dropping the small circles onto a cookie sheet. "Yeah," he replied. "It's an Evergreen tradition."

Hannah stepped in between them, a container of milk in one hand and a canister to put cookies inside in the other. Farther down at the other end of the island, Meg measured out flour, and behind her, Elliot removed another piping hot batch of cookie goodness from the oven.

"We ran out of these for the Christmas Festival one year," Hannah replied, "and that party requires a lot of cookies, so now—"

"Baking parties are happening all over town, actually," Michelle chimed in when she stepped up at the opposite side of the island.

"And on today's agenda, the perfect chocolate chip cookie," Meg said, taking the tray from Elliot to hold up as a display.

Ezra immediately stepped up next to her to take a cookie from the tray. Hannah grinned as he tossed the hot cookie from one hand to the next, refusing to put it down because he couldn't wait to taste it.

Sonya stood looking around the kitchen, her furrowed brow sending the message that she still wasn't convinced this was such a good idea.

"It's a lot of fun if you just loosen up a little," Michelle told Sonya playfully. Sonya pretended to toss some of the chips at her sister, but then smiled in response to Michelle's comment.

"Hannah, did you know that Megan does a holiday cocktail hour every night here at the Inn? With carols?" Ezra asked.

Megan chuckled. "It was her idea!"

Hannah shrugged. "People come to Evergreen for the Christmas spirit; I figured we might as well go way over the top."

At the other end of the island, Zoe spooned measured amounts of sugar into a bowl. "That should be the town slogan," she added with a chuckle.

"I heard that," Michelle said while pouring the chocolate chips into the mixer. "And I'll consider it."

As Christmas carols played from a radio somewhere in the kitchen, Hannah joined Elliot at the sink where he was drying off more cookie sheets. She'd picked up a cookie on the way and broke a piece off. Since his hands were wet, she happily placed the piece of cookie in his mouth. He chewed, grinning at her as he did so. She popped a piece into her mouth. "So good," she said.

"Always," he replied, and dried his hands on a towel before brushing his fingers over her cheek.

"So, Zoe," Michelle continued. "Where are your parents?" The question was spoken in French, but Zoe replied in English.

"Well, it looks like my dad's not going to make it for Christmas. His partner's wife went into labor, so

Dad has to be on call at the medical center now. Allie's a little crushed, and so am I." She managed a tentative smile. "But I'll see him when we get back."

Michelle crossed over to her then, and put an arm around her. "Well, that just means you get to celebrate Christmas twice."

Hannah and Elliot had finished their first cookie and moved on to the second while standing close, both looking at Zoe. She'd been thinking of what her and Elliot's children would be like as she watched Zoe and David move about the kitchen.

Did Elliot ever think along those same lines?

Well, of course he did. They both loved being with David, so it would make sense that they'd want their own children one day. And Elliot held a craft class for the kindergartners at the elementary school once a month.

She heard a phone ring and saw Elliot reach into his back pocket to grab it. "Excuse me, babe," he said, while still chewing the cookie they were sharing.

Something about the way Elliot had looked down at the phone screen before he'd told her he had to take the call made Hannah a little nervous. It was just a brief flutter in the pit of her stomach, but as she watched him move quickly into the other room, she couldn't help but wonder who was on the other end of that phone.

"Come on, Hannah, we need more chips over here," Zoe said, and Hannah stopped looking toward the doorway Elliot had just walked through.

Instead, she turned her attention back to the cookie baking and the good time she was having with friends.

"Jingle Bells" was playing now, and she, Zoe and David sang as she poured more chocolate chips into the bowl. They all laughed when she stopped to pop a few into her mouth.

The song was over by the time Elliot came back into the kitchen, touching her elbow as he walked by. "Hey," he said, looking at her with a strange expression on his face.

"Uh, who was that?" she asked, unable to let the uneasy sensation rest.

"Oh, that was the people who…uh, I got the money from the foundation," he announced, excitement clear in his tone.

Hannah was momentarily speechless. Then managed to whisper, "Really?"

"Wait," Ezra said, coming over to place a hand on Elliot's shoulder. "You got it?"

Grinning and still holding his phone in one hand, Elliot replied, "Yeah!"

"Elliot, that's wonderful," Ezra said, looking from Elliot to Hannah and then back to Elliot again.

"They said that my application had the most charm. That since Evergreen was already such a Christmas destination, it made sense that people would flock to a shop that embodies everything that we do best."

The heavy sense of dread that had overcome her the moment he made that announcement was almost too much for Hannah to bear. She felt horrible that she didn't share his enthusiasm. Still, she managed a smile as she removed her apron and leaned in to give him a hug.

"That's great," she said, wrapping her arms around him. But there was no happiness in her tone. She couldn't find any, not when getting this loan meant that Elliot would open another Tinker Shop…in the city.

"Congratulations," she said to him when they pulled apart. "I'm so happy for you and I hope it's everything you wanted." There was truth to her words, even though it pained her to say them. "Um, but I'd better head back to the museum if I'm gonna get it open on time."

"Hey, do you want some help?" Elliot asked. "We could continue our day together."

"No, you stay here. Celebrate," she told him, and then moved away. "All right, guys, bye."

Hannah couldn't wait to get out of that kitchen and away from Elliot. But even after she'd put on her coat and stepped outside into the brisk afternoon breeze, the heaviness in the center of her chest was still there. The feeling that she couldn't now, nor would she ever be able to take another deep breath without feeling that pain front and center, weighed heavily on her. Elliot was going to open another Tinker Shop in Boston. What did that mean for their relationship?

Michelle had just accepted a FaceTime call from Thomas as she spotted Hannah walking out of the Inn. She hadn't waved or said goodbye because she was too busy smiling at her husband-to-be. Her destination was the front room of the Inn so she could have some privacy for the call.

"Hey, Michelle," Thomas said the moment she answered.

"Hey, sweetie, how's it going?" She sat in front of the fireplace holding the phone up so she could see him. "Any news?"

"I, um, I'm so sorry but, um…the storm has us trapped," he said.

Oh, no. Michelle's heart sank. Her worst fears were coming to fruition. Without his even saying the words, she knew what was coming, and dread settled over her like a cloak.

"I hate to say this, but I don't think I'm gonna make it back for the rehearsal," Thomas continued. He shook his head. "It doesn't look good."

"Well, is there any way they could plow?" Reaching for hope was instinctual. This wedding meant so much to her. Sure, they'd decided that it would be small and intimate, but that in no way minimized how monumental exchanging their vows was going to be.

"Oh, honey, believe me, we have tried everything that we can. I've never seen snow like this. Now we've managed to get a lot of people up the hill, but even if I—"

"No, no, no, be safe," she told him. Mentally scolding herself for letting her emotions take precedence, she wanted to be clear that she didn't want anyone in danger because of her desire for this wedding to happen. "Whatever has to be done to keep everyone safe. That's what I want." And she meant those words, no matter how much saying them still pricked her heart.

Thomas looked away from the screen. "Michelle, listen, I gotta go. I'll call you back, okay?"

"Okay. Okay. No problem. Be safe." She sighed. "I'll talk to you tomorrow. I love you."

"I love you too," he replied, and she disconnected the call.

After watching him disappear from the screen, Michelle held the phone tightly in her hands. She dropped her head and sighed heavily, wondering what she was going to do now. If Thomas couldn't make it home for the rehearsal, what were the odds he'd be back for the wedding? Shaking her head, she knew there was nothing she could do to change the circumstances, and neither could Thomas. If he were here with her, they'd be wishing for snow on their wedding day, so she couldn't bring herself to curse the weather and its bad timing in Maine at this moment.

That didn't mean she had to like the situation. On a deep huff, she rested her elbows on her knee. She didn't much feel like going back to the cookie-baking party. Sitting with the phone clenched in her hands, she rocked back and forth, saying a silent prayer for Thomas and his staff to remain safe, but also for him to get home in time for their wedding.

Chapter Twelve

At the museum, Hannah continued to work to keep her mind off what was going on with Elliot. Running all the facts through her mind wasn't going to do her any good. She still didn't understand how they'd gotten to this point.

Never, in all the time they'd been together—even just as friends—had Elliot ever mentioned wanting to go back to live in the city. She'd thought he was just as happy as she was living in Evergreen.

Her hands shook as she placed them on the ladder and she paused, taking a deep, steadying breath. The last thing she needed to do was take a tumble from the top of a ladder because she was distracted by thoughts of her boyfriend. Besides, thinking about the issues with Elliot weren't going to change his plans. Hannah didn't think anything was going to do that. And she'd never ask him to. Not if this was definitely what he wanted to do, which it seemed to be. Her wish for Elliot was always going to be be, first and foremost, his happiness. If he was no longer happy here in Evergreen—with her—then she'd have to find some way to accept that.

In the next seconds, she felt steadier, and she climbed up on the ladder, placing more bulbs on the garland that hung over the walkway leading from one exhibit hall to the next.

"Hannah?" She heard Elliot's voice seconds after she'd placed the final bulb.

Taking steady steps to get down off the ladder, she looked over her shoulder just in time to see Elliot rounding the corner to where she was. "I thought you were staying behind to celebrate."

"I was just so excited," he said. "I wanted to be here with you, to tell you about the—"

"Yeah," she said, cutting him off. "I suppose we should have that conversation, huh."

"It's gonna be amazing. We take everything that the Tinker Shop has ended up becoming, and then some. The art classes, the ornaments that people make, the Kringle Cookbook! Everything unique." His excitement was evident in the vibrant way in which he spoke each word. The light that showed in his eyes and the huge grin on his face.

How could she love him so much and not share this joy with him? But how could she be happy about something that could potentially tear them apart?

"Everything unique about the Evergreen lifestyle," she murmured when she felt guilty enough to speak.

"Exactly." Elliot looked around, opening his arms to their surroundings before letting them drop back to his side. "People come to Evergreen for all this magic.

The Tinker Shop here will stay open, but we'll have a flagship store in Boston. Rebrand it. I can finally take you up on your suggestion of changing the name."

When she'd suggested the name change, she hadn't thought it would mean a location change as well. She felt as confused as she was dejected. "To what?"

"The Turner Goods Company," he replied dramatically. He even used his hands to make a motion like the new name was appearing on an imaginary display.

Hannah couldn't help it; she chuckled. That was perhaps the only thing keeping her from crying. "Wow, that's a really smart plan. I mean—"

He didn't let her finish but stepped closer to take her hands. "Come with me."

This moment had come a lot sooner than she'd thought it would. And she was actually a little shocked. Each time she'd let thoughts of Elliot and this second shop filter through her mind, it had been with the notion that he'd be leaving Evergreen. It hadn't occurred to her that he would ask her to go with him. Maybe because she'd never entertained any thoughts of leaving her hometown. On one hand, she supposed she should feel flattered that he wanted her with him, that he thought of this as something they could do together, but Hannah couldn't leave Evergreen. This was where she belonged.

"Elliot, I love everything I'm doing at the Christmas Museum," she told him, and that part was true. She couldn't explain how being here and planning for this museum to open made her feel inside. It was so different from any of the other jobs she'd ever done.

Her heart sank when he looked totally depleted by her words.

"I thought this would excite you," he said.

She gripped his hand tighter. "It does. I'm really excited for you," she said, knowing that deep down inside her words were true. "But where does that leave us if we want different things?"

This too was a hard question, one she'd pushed to the back of her mind many times in the past couple of days. The heavy feeling in her chest signaled she still wasn't ready to hear it, nor was she prepared for whatever his answer was going to be.

When Elliot didn't immediately respond, Hannah felt worse.

The sound of someone clearing their throat pulled their attention away from each other and they looked toward the entryway to see who the new visitor was.

"Oh, Mr. Cooper? What brings you back?" Although he was the absolute last person Hannah wanted to see, she'd slipped right into her cheerful tone.

Jeb took off his hat and walked toward her. "I own one third of this building."

If there was anything she wasn't in the mood to deal with right now, it was Jeb Cooper and his unwavering resistance to everything she was trying to do with the museum.

Moving around, staring at every decoration as if he couldn't wait to tear it down, Jeb stopped a few feet away from her. "I spoke with some members of the town council. They provided me with a copy of the contract my sisters signed, turning this building over to the town."

He seemed oddly pleased by what he was saying and Hannah knew that was cause for alarm. "Is there a problem with that?"

"I told you," he said, stepping closer again. "I did not give my permission."

Hannah felt her world spinning out of control. All of this could not be happening in the same night, it just couldn't.

"Okay, let's look at this realistically, Mr. Cooper," Elliot began. "I'm sure if you're looking to negotiate new terms for the use of this building that the town council can work that out with you."

Right. She should've said that. She was responsible for the museum, not Elliot. "Or if you'd like to take a tour with me, we can discuss some of the things you'd like to see here."

"That's just it," Jeb continued. "There's nothing here I'd like to see. None of it. I'd rather have the building stand empty than to have people traipsing all around staring and talking."

"But Mr. Cooper, it's a good thing if people are talking about how great Evergreen is."

"It's never a good thing to be talked about, Ms. Turner. Never," he snapped, and then, as was proving customary for him, he walked away.

"I can't believe this," Hannah said, bringing her hands up to cover her face. She huffed out a breath and felt comforted by Elliot's hands on her shoulders.

"Just breathe," he said. "This is going to get worked out."

She sure hoped he was right. It felt good to have Elliot by her side and standing up for her. Unfortunately, it wasn't a feeling that could last for long, not with his plan to move to Boston.

It was early the next morning when Elliot walked up to the door at the Tinker Shop. He hadn't slept very well last night so he'd been dragging a little, but he'd wanted to stop by Hannah's house first to talk to her again. When David had told him she'd already left, he'd known he would find her here.

Elliot didn't open the door right away. He just stood there, watching her through the window, thinking the same thoughts that had plagued him most of last night. How was he going to do this without her? And did he really want to?

No, he didn't. Every plan he'd made had always been with the thought that she'd be right by his side. He'd never once considered that she wouldn't go with him. Well, that wasn't entirely true. If he was honest with himself, which he resigned himself to being this morning when his conscience had enough time to drum this into his system—he'd known all about Hannah's love for Evergreen.

It was part of why he loved her so much: the way she loved others and this place they all called home. She was an admirable woman, a treasure he didn't want to lose. But how could he keep her and still follow his dreams? Could he convince her to go with him, and if he did, would she resent him later? For all the time he'd spent hammering out the details of the business plan that had gotten him the loan, he hadn't taken nearly enough time to think through how this would actually impact their relationship.

With a heavy sigh he touched the doorknob, turned it slowly and stepped inside. The bells overhead jingled, but Hannah didn't look up. She was sitting in a chair in front of the grandfather clock, knitting.

Closing the door behind him, Elliot looked over at her again. This was the woman he loved, the lovely lady dressed in black ankle boots, jeans, a black t-shirt and a warm gray sweater, with pockets. Hannah needed all her pockets for holding pens, rolls of tape, extra buttons. Anything she could think of or saw on the floor or somewhere it wasn't supposed to be ended up in one of her pockets to take care of later.

He liked her hair in the braided style; he also liked when it had been straight and hanging down her back. He adored her smile, which she wasn't doing now, and the way her eyes lit up each time she saw or even thought about anything having to do with Christmas. His heart ached with the thought that he might not see or experience any of these things again.

"Early start," he said, after he figured he'd stood there staring at her long enough.

Hannah's response was a yawn as she continued knitting. She looked so peaceful sitting in the Tinker

Shop where she belonged. That thought scraped along every plan he had for himself, a painful reminder of her question last night and his inability, or hesitance, to answer.

"Excuse me," she said, dropping her hands into her lap. "I couldn't sleep."

Elliot wanted to tell her that he hadn't slept much last night either, but he didn't. There always seemed to be so much he wanted to say to Hannah, but even more that he never did.

She sighed as he removed his scarf and coat and hung them on the rack.

"I mean, just with all of Mr. Cooper's demands, the choir, all of it. And as much as I appreciate Zoe's help, knitting calms me down. It was the same for my mother." She looked as if she were thinking about those last words for a few moments and he used that time to get his thoughts together. "And I know we have a lot to talk about and I know getting the funding is a big deal, I just—"

"I know," he said, feeling the weight of guilt resting on his shoulders. The pain of her possibly not going to Boston with him had settled deep in his chest, but he was trying valiantly to ignore it. "You have so much on your plate, so I know this is not the best timing, but, Hannah, honey, I want to do this." He knelt down on the floor so they could be eye to eye, saying the words he'd thought about all night. "And we should talk about—"

"We should talk about what, Elliot? About how you expect me to walk away from everything I know and love, to go somewhere I've never been, and open your new store?" She sighed.

"It would be your store too, Hannah. It would be ours, something we built together." He took her hand even though she still held the knitting needle. "I know that you and I have made some really good changes here in the past months, but in the end the Tinker Shop is still really the Turner Tinker Shop. People in town know about it because of your parents; a lot of them continue to bring their things here for me to tinker with because they remember your parents."

He knew it sounded selfish and ungrateful, but there were things inside him that were just pouring out now. Elliot didn't know how to stop them, nor did he know if they were helping or hurting his case.

"I just want something that we've built from start to finish," he said. Something that he could also say he'd done without the benefit of his businessman father's tutelage.

It was that last part that held Elliot still as he waited to see what Hannah would say next. His father hadn't been there for Elliot, not when Elliot discovered his joy in fixing and creating things or when he'd decided to buy the Tinker Shop and become a business owner. The thought had never occurred to Elliot before, but now, it was starting to sink in that maybe he was trying to prove a point. That after all these years without his father's presence in his life, he'd still made something of himself.

He didn't have to wait much longer for Hannah's

response because in the next seconds, the bells above the door were ringing again as students for the pottery class came filing into the shop.

"Hi—good morning." Hannah sat up straighter in the chair and waved to them.

Knowing he needed to act as normal as possible, Elliot lifted a hand to wave as well.

"Shall we, uh…"

"Pick this up later." He finished her sentence and watched her begin putting her knitting stuff away.

"Yeah," Hannah replied with a slow nod.

Elliot wanted to talk this through right now. He wanted to make Hannah understand why this meant so much to him and to convince her that coming with him would be good for both of him, but now just wasn't the time.

※

"I'm sorry, I'm a being a downer," Hannah said, minutes after she'd taken a seat at the table for her scheduled brunch with Michelle and Sonya.

Today's get-together had been pre-planned before Elliot's announcement at the cookie baking party last night, and Michelle had texted Hannah earlier this morning to confirm. Hannah had stared at her phone for endless seconds, debating whether or not to bail on the meet-up. In the end, she hadn't been able to do it, no matter how bad she was feeling.

And, as a result, here she was dumping all her issues with Elliot onto these two women who probably thought they were here to discuss wedding stuff.

"It's just that I don't know what to do. All this seemed to come out of the blue with Elliot. I mean, when was he going to tell me he didn't want to live in Evergreen? Here I was thinking I might be the next one in line to get a Christmas proposal, and this happens. And to top all that off, Mr. Cooper won't give us permission to use the old Hat Factory for the Christmas Museum." She sighed. "I'm babbling, aren't I?"

Sonya nodded. "But it's okay, girl, you let it all out."

Michelle picked up her mug and took a sip. "She's right. We're here for you, Hannah, so you go right ahead and tell us everything that's on your mind."

"Well, first, before you get into that, let me tell you about Jeb Cooper," Michelle said. "He's right. We don't have ownership of the building, and in order to get his signature, he has a few demands."

Hannah groaned. "Don't remind me. He wants a cut of the gift shop sales; he wants us to give him half of the admission fees. I was copied on the email he wrote to the town council."

"The council will work it out," Michelle said with a wave of her hand. "But we got him to agree you can move ahead while we do that."

"Well, at least that's something," Hannah replied.

"Now, back to your guy trouble," Sonya said. "That's way more interesting than Mr. Scrooge."

Hannah managed to smile, even though she really should be tired of thinking about her guy trouble. But Michelle and Sonya were being so sweet to her and

Hannah was being a whiner—or was she? Actually, she felt a little more angry than whiny.

"I mean, am I wrong? Should I just be happy that Elliot even thought about me in this process and pick up all my roots and leave the only home I've ever known?"

"If you love him," Michelle said.

"Absolutely not," Sonya replied at the same time.

Hannah sat across the table from them, starring from one to the other. The Cooper sisters they certainly were not. Michelle and Sonya's personalities were almost as different as night and day, with Michelle's pleasant vibe and Sonya's prickly demeanor. Still, there was a closeness there; it was easy to see with the way they just gave each other a look that kind of told the other to be quiet. Hannah smiled weakly. "Okay, that's good advice."

Michelle shook her head. "What I'm saying is that change can be good, Hannah. Look, I never thought about finding love again. After the last flop of a relationship I had two years ago, I was content living my best life as the mayor. Then Thomas came along and everything I thought I was fine without became a necessity, because it was coming from him. Do you get what I'm sayin'?"

Sonya had ordered the eggnog waffles and she used the time while Michelle was talking to cut into them and stuff a bite into her mouth. She was just finishing chewing when her sister finished. "I can see that," she said to Hannah and Michelle's dismay. "But listen, you have a right to your own life too. Now, if Elliot had talked to you about these plans beforehand, maybe the two of you could've worked out a compromise."

"They could still work out a compromise," Michelle said. "Whereas there's no compromise in Thomas being stuck in Maine for our rehearsal dinner."

"Oh Michelle, that's right. David told me when I got home that his father wasn't going to make it back in time for the rehearsal dinner. I'm so sorry. I've been sitting here going on and on about my personal stuff like it's anything in comparison to what you're going through."

"No, no, listening to you talk kind of took my mind off the wedding that might not happen."

It was Sonya's turn to shake her head.

"So, Ebenezer Scrooge wants to change your plans for the museum?" Sonya asked, circling back to Hannah's earlier comment about Mr. Cooper.

Michelle held her mug in both hands and took another sip. "Which is frustrating because both sisters are fine with it."

Sonya continued, pointing her fork across the table at Hannah. "And your boyfriend wants to move to Boston."

Hannah nodded. "Yup."

"Your husband-to-be is stuck in Maine days before your wedding," Sonya continued, looking over at Michelle again. With a scoff she sat back in her chair. "Anyone else having any holiday-themed problems?" she asked, her voice growing slightly louder so that other patrons at the Kringle could hear her.

Carol sailed by wearing a black wool coat and red turtleneck. "Well, my son-in-law's trapped in Paris," she added, and paused only long enough for Michelle to offer a consolatory nod.

Sonya continued with an amused look on her face. "This town has some very unique sadnesses."

"Well, Thomas and I have our whole lives together, so I probably should call Henry Miller and cancel the rehearsal dinner," Michelle said.

Dour looks were exchanged around the table as Hannah searched for something comforting to say. She really did feel bad for Michelle and couldn't imagine keeping such a brave face if she were in her position. But try as she might, she couldn't find any consolation to offer, possibly because she wasn't feeling comforted herself. In fact, she was more out of sorts than she ever recalled being in her life.

"But on the plus side," Michelle continued, "I'll have a little more time to work with you, Hannah."

"Actually, would you mind if I kept doing this myself?" Hannah asked. The one thing she had right now that was bringing her joy was the museum, and she didn't want Michelle to think she couldn't handle it on her own.

Michelle frowned. "What do you mean?"

"Well, I like the Christmas Museum job. I just need to figure out how you do it. Stay calm when there's so much to do."

"I learned how," Michelle said with a nod. "Yeah, remember when I used to run around this town trying to get a Christmas Festival together? And when they changed the venue one year I had a full-out panic attack over cookies?"

Hannah tried to stifle her grin. "Yeah, I remember that."

"Well, I wasn't here, so do tell," Sonya said.

Michelle waved a hand at her sister. "Sometimes when we slow down, we learn how to manage—how to sort out what's important, what we want."

"Yeah," Hannah said, giving Michelle's words some thought. "With all that I do, I've never had one thing that I could sacrifice the others for. It's like you just said, I think I've finally figured out the one thing that's important to me." She took a deep breath and released it slowly, resigned to the decision she'd just made. "I want to see this through."

"Well, I suppose," Michelle started, and Hannah held her breath. "I gave you the job, so it's yours."

Beaming, Hannah replied, "Thank you." She took one last sip of coffee before standing. "Now, I have a ton of work to do. But first, I have to let go of a thing or two." She put on her coat and waved goodbye.

Chapter Thirteen

Michelle and Sonya were still sitting at the table minutes after Hannah left when a familiar voice came with a chuckle.

"Ladies, look what Santa brought you." Michelle looked up to see Gordon Lansing walking toward the table, arms outstretched, huge grin on his face. His cap of snow-white hair and infectious smile were a sight that pierced Michelle's heart.

She jumped right up, skirting around the table to throw her arms around her father. "Daddy!" She closed her eyes, loving the familiar scent of Old Spice cologne he always wore. "Classic, you just showing up like that," she said before releasing him.

Sonya stood too, but she didn't hug Gordon. With sadness, Michelle observed the resigned look the two of them shared.

"I asked where to find the mayor, and was told to check here by a jolly old man who looks surprisingly like—" He let his words trail off with a skeptical look.

Michelle continued, "A broad face, round little belly,

shakes when he laughs like a bowl full of—"

"Hangs around chimneys? Lives up north? You know the type," Sonya finished, and had them all laughing.

"Yeah, Nick," Michelle added finally. "He's around here somewhere."

The Lansing trio stood laughing together in a way Michelle had missed for far too long. She couldn't wait to hear all about her father's trip and spend some much-needed time with him. But before she could invite him to sit down and join them, a woman who looked to be close to her father's age, with short cropped blonde hair, came up behind him. With a cheerful smile, she hooked her arm in Gordon's and Michelle watched as her father turned to this woman and shared an adoring grin with her.

Oh? Well, okay, this was unexpected. There was no laughing at this point as Michelle tried to wrap her mind around what was going on.

"Michelle," Gordon said, most likely seeing the confusion on his youngest daughter's face. "I'd like you to meet Bea."

And just like that, Michelle knew exactly what was going on. Her father was dating this woman named Bea. Beside her Sonya had tensed, and they were all staring at Michelle as if waiting to see what her reaction would be. It'd been two years since her mother's death, and in that time she hadn't heard anything about her father dating anyone else. Now here he was, looking as pleased as punch to have this lady named Bea by his side.

"Oh, well, hi, Bea. Nice to meet you." As mayor

of the town, Michelle was used to smiling cordially and shaking hands, so she did the same with Bea, even while her feelings about this new development were still dancing in shock.

"It's wonderful to meet you, Michelle," Bea said while shaking her hand. "And you must be Sonya." Bea wore a rust-colored coat and gold knot earrings; her smile was warm and welcoming.

And Gordon looked absolutely smitten with her. He stood with his arm around Bea, his thin-framed black glasses perched high up on his nose. And, if Michelle wasn't mistaken, there was a little puff to his chest as if he was just as proud to be making this introduction as he was of everything Michelle or Sonya had ever done.

Speaking of Sonya, she didn't shake Bea's hand. Bea must've anticipated that because she hadn't offered her hand either, but instead gave Sonya an understanding glance. Michelle was glad to see that Sonya did at least offer Bea a smile.

"I've heard such great things about both of you," Bea continued. "Beautiful little town you have here."

"Oh, the town's all hers," Sonya replied with a nod to Michelle.

"Shall we get some lunch?" Gordon suggested.

"Sure, have a seat," Michelle said, directing her father and Bea toward the table where she and Sonya had been seated.

"So," Sonya said in an undertone. "That's Bea, Dad's new girlfriend."

"Well, she seems lovely," Michelle responded, noting

the skeptical look on Sonya's face. "Oh, wait a minute. Is this what your little tiff with Dad is all about?"

Without a qualm, Sonya nodded. "It absolutely is."

Spending time with Michelle and Sonya today had been just what Hannah needed. Both women had given her good advice about how to deal with the Mr. Cooper and Elliot situations. And more importantly, Michelle's wise words had steered Hannah in the direction she needed to go for herself.

In the past few days, Hannah had been giving a lot of thought to her busy schedule and how it was affecting her life here in Evergreen. The life she'd been happily living until a few unplanned things had been tossed in the mix. Growing up, there'd never been a doubt in Hannah's mind that she would fall in love, get married and have children, all while doing whatever she could to help the people and the town of Evergreen. And every day she'd felt as if she was taking one more step toward that goal, especially when she fell in love with Elliot. What had never occurred to her was the time and energy maintaining a healthy relationship entailed—that wasn't something she'd paid very much attention to where her parents were concerned.

Barbara and Isaac were just a steadfast and dependable staple in Hannah's life. They loved each other, their children and their town. Hannah, like most children, hadn't thought about how or why that came to be. She also never wondered how her parents managed to juggle all the things they did in town while raising two kids and building a happy home. She'd just assumed that when the time came, she'd be able to pull it off too. Now, she was beginning to see things differently. She was starting to feel like she needed a little more focus and a lot fewer assignments. Not just to work on her relationship with Elliot—no, that was going along its own path, which she knew they'd have to deal with sooner rather than later. But what she'd decided to do to get her life in order was prioritize and trim where needed.

Now, with a plan in mind, Hannah ran across the Town Square when she spotted Carol.

"Carol! Carol, wait up!" she yelled, dodging in and out of a group of people who'd just come from the bakery.

Carol heard her and slowed down, rubbing her hands together against the afternoon chill. "Oh, hey Hannah. Just heading over to choir practice."

"That's actually what I wanted to talk to you about," Hannah said.

"Yeah? What's going on? New music you have in mind?"

Hannah shook her head. "Better. How would you feel about taking over the choir?" The look of surprise on Carol's face gave no clue as to whether she would agree or not.

"What?"

They'd stepped up onto the curb now, standing near one of the lampposts that had been neatly wrapped in red, gold and green ribbon.

"You were right the other day when you reminded me to be open to help," Hannah said. "So, here I am now, asking if you'd like to help with the choir."

"Oh, honey, come on. I didn't mean that you needed to give something up."

"Well, if it's too much, I understand. But you've been a part of the choir your whole life. You know the music and you have experience." Hannah presented her case for why Carol was the best option for the job. She was amazed at how quickly she'd decided to ask her and that she knew exactly whom to ask in the first place. Maybe she'd always known in the back of her mind that somebody else could do the job just as well as she did.

"Well, I can't deny this would be a great way to try something new," Carol said.

Filled with hope once more, Hannah smiled. "Well, then, the choir's yours, if you'd like it?"

"Yes!" Carol said, still a bit hesitantly.

"Yes?"

"I would!" Carol grinned and reached out a hand for Hannah to shake. "Deal!"

"How long have Dad and Bea been a thing?" Michelle asked Sonya later that afternoon. She'd been watching her father with his new friend at lunch and now as they checked into a room at the Inn. Gordon had been attentive to Bea, helping her with her coat, handing her cream and sugar for her coffee. While Bea had laughed at Gordon's corny jokes and patted the back of his hand whenever he looked worried at something Sonya said. They seemed to be really happy, and that made Michelle happy.

"You know, it's unclear. He didn't say. But as soon as he told me, I put my foot down immediately. And said it's inappropriate to dishonor our mother's memory by inviting his new girlfriend to his daughter's wedding. I defended you."

Michelle looked at her sister with surprise. Sonya may've been a pain while they were growing up, but she'd never been so vehement about anything when it came to their parents. "Defended me? What are you talking about? Yes, I would've liked a heads up, but I know he's not good at talking about emotions, let alone a new romance. I can cut him some slack. You know, you also could've told me; I'm a big girl."

Sonya scoffed, and Michelle was about to really get into the conversation about minding their own business and staying out of their father's love life, when her ringing phone interrupted them. With a frown at Sonya, she looked down at her phone, and felt at ease the moment she saw Thomas's name on the screen.

"I'll be right back; don't you say another unpleasant word to either Daddy or Bea," she told Sonya before leaving her sister at the front desk.

As soon as Michelle accepted the call, she noted how stressed Thomas looked. He wasn't smiling and his shoulders were slumped as he sat on a couch. Behind him there was a window and through it she could see the weather hadn't changed much. "How's it going up there?" she asked, the moment she sat on the couch in the front room.

"Worse and worse," he replied to her dismay. "Not only is the snow still coming down, but the forecast for the next week isn't looking good."

"Well, do you think you'll get out at all? I mean, in time for the wedding?" This had been all Michelle could think about since Thomas told her he wouldn't make it back in time for the rehearsal. While a part of her had tried to hold out hope, dread still circled in the pit of her stomach.

"Michelle, at this rate, I don't even know if I can get us all out for Christmas."

Every fear she'd been harboring for the last couple of days rested on her shoulders with his words, and all Michelle could do was close her eyes to the wave of sadness.

"Honey, I am…" Thomas paused, his voice filling with emotion. "I am so sorry. I tried so hard."

Opening her eyes again she took a deep breath. "Look, Thomas," she started, but he interrupted.

"It's our wedding," he said insistently. "This time it's different."

"I know, I know," she told him. "But still, sometimes you gotta stay put to stay safe." No matter how smart those words sounded, the disappointment was clear by the look on Thomas's face and the heaviness in the center of her chest. "It's not forever. Me and you, we're forever. Not being able to travel, that'll be over one day."

"Is that my future son-in-law?" Gordon asked,

coming into the room to sit quickly beside Michelle.

"Look, Dad, it's not a good—" Michelle started to say, but her father was already leaning in.

"Looking forward to seeing you, son," Gordon said, in a much louder tone than was necessary.

"You too, sir," Thomas replied. "It's just, ah, I'm afraid the forecast doesn't look very promising."

Before he could say another word, the connection began to fail and the screen on Michelle's phone froze. "Thomas? Thomas?"

When the screen went blank, Michelle lowered her hands to her lap. "Change of plans," she said, looking up to see that Sonya and Bea had joined them.

Chapter Fourteen

Hannah's last stop before going home for the evening was the Christmas Museum. She'd left some boxes of old postcards she wanted to organize into a collage and Elliot was going to help her load them in the truck and bring them home. When she arrived, Hannah went through the back door because it was easier to park the truck on that side. She was removing her scarf and walking past some old storage space when she heard something.

Doubling back, she paused when she saw the door was cracked, and she leaned forward to peek inside.

Mr. Cooper!

It was a jolt seeing him inside the tiny room that appeared to be filled with old hats. He wasn't wearing his normal black fedora, but his shoulders were slumped as usual, the look on his face grim. What could've happened to this man to make him as unhappy as he always appeared? She had no clue, but wished there was something she could do for him. Not just because she needed his cooperation to see this museum through to fruition, but because she genuinely hated seeing anyone as distressed as Jeb Cooper always looked.

When he began to turn around, Hannah ducked back, tiptoeing away from the door until she was around the corner. A few moments later, and she saw Elliot stepping back from the wall where it appeared he'd just hung another picture.

"Hey," she whispered, walking up to him. "Mr. Cooper is in the back room. I thought it was just storage, but it's full of…" She stopped talking the moment Elliot looked at her.

His lips were drawn in a tight line, his gaze somber. He didn't respond to what she'd said, but instead moved to sit down on the edge of the platform behind him. He rested his elbows on his legs and stared straight ahead.

"What's wrong?" Hannah asked.

"I don't like the way we keep leaving things," he said solemnly and glanced over at her.

Folding her coat to place on the ledge, Hannah sat down beside him. "Yeah, me neither." And she'd known that this moment was going to come whether she wanted it to or not. "Look," she continued, looping her arm into his. "I just wish that you had told me sooner that you were planning this big thing."

Would that have made a difference? Probably not, but it would've at least made her feel like she was a part of his decision to make such a huge move.

"Yeah, I know. I should've." He shrugged. "Guess I wasn't sure how you'd react even then."

"I don't want you to ever feel like you can't tell me

something because you're worried about my reaction. You always used to confide in me before, so it was hard to hear this news the way I did." Speaking those words out loud confirmed how disappointed she really was by that part of Elliot's plan.

Nodding, he lifted his hands and dragged them over his face. "You're right, and for that I apologize. I just wanted to wait until I knew more." He sighed. "With every step I took in this process, I thought about you. About what this would mean for us. But honestly, would you have come with me if I'd asked you sooner?"

Hannah heard everything he'd just said, but in doing so she wondered if Elliot had ever really known her at all. If he did, wouldn't he have already known the answer to that question? There was an earnestness to his tone that Hannah had never heard before. And he watched her, waiting for her to respond. The way he blinked slowly and shook his head said he knew what her answer was going to be.

"Probably not," she whispered. "No." It had to be said, for both of them. "I think I've always been searching for my purpose here in Evergreen. Even when I didn't really know it." She tucked a few wayward braids behind her ear. "But when I walked into this museum I knew I'd found it…and now, I want to see it through." She cleared her throat. "I mean, it's something I need to do, for me."

Elliot sat perfectly still, staring straight ahead once more. She didn't know what he was thinking. For once in the history of their friendship, she couldn't imagine what he was going to say next.

"I think your idea is really smart," she continued, when the silence seemed to build like a mountain between them.

The grin he gave her came with a restless sigh.

"And I think it could work well and I don't want you to regret not doing it," She continued. The need to tell him everything she was feeling at this moment was potent. She didn't want there to be any more secrets between them, no more miscommunications.

He stood, the movement restless and anxious. "Hannah, this isn't just about the business," he implored. "I wanna meet the Hannah and Elliot who live in the city."

And who was that exactly? She had no idea—she only knew what she felt. "But I love the Hannah and Elliot who live here," she told him.

Squeezing the bridge of his nose, he closed his eyes for a beat and then looked at her again. "I just wonder if maybe we need to shake things up a bit."

Hannah stood now, staring at him with what she expected was the same confused look she was feeling. "You said 'we.' Do 'we' need to shake things up, or do you?"

Now she was just a few feet away from him, but it felt like there was an entire world between them. Something about what he'd just said was shedding a new light on this whole scenario. Had Elliot been thinking he wanted something different than what they had? She swallowed the urge to sob.

"Because I know who I am, Elliot, and I know what I want. My life and everything I love is here in Evergreen. This community has and will always be my family. And honestly, I thought you felt the same way. I thought we both wanted to build our future here."

A sharp pain pierced her chest as she watched his brow furrow and she realized she'd been wrong all along.

Elliot shook his head. "I know what you want to hear," he started. "What everyone in town has always thought. Yes, my mother had visited Evergreen when she was young and when she and my father divorced she wanted to come back here. She was happy here," he said.

"But you weren't? Not even when we were growing up together, you weren't happy."

"No," he immediately replied. "I mean, yes, yes I was. Every day that I could be with you made me happy, Hannah. Never doubt that, not from the beginning up until this point. But there's more. My mother came here to hide, and I want to go back to the city to live."

If a ton of bricks had fallen on her at this moment, Hannah couldn't have been more hurt. There was also disappointment in the fact that she'd believed in a dream—love, marriage and family with Elliot—that had never really had a chance. Because as long as he'd wanted to be somewhere other than Evergreen, he'd be choosing not to be with her.

Hannah sighed and looked away. She took a slow breath and told herself she could look at him again. She could say what needed to be said, and then walk away from him knowing she'd given this all she had.

"We went into this saying that we would be friends no matter what," she told him. "Maybe we should spend some time apart and figure out what we want as individuals."

The quick widening of his eyes followed by a frown pierced her soul. He stepped toward her as if he were going to reach out and touch or possibly hug her. She couldn't take that right now. If he hugged her she might break, and that was the last thing Hannah wanted to do.

Elliot stopped the moment she moved away from him. "Hannah. Are you sure?"

"Are *you* sure, Elliot? Is everything that you want in Boston more important than what you have right here?"

He opened his mouth to say something, but then quickly closed it again.

She nodded, blinking rapidly to keep the tears that threatened to fall away. "It's okay to have a dream and to want to fulfill that dream. I have things I want to do too. They're just here, in Evergreen."

"Hannah," he said again, but she knew nothing was going to change.

"Goodnight, Elliot," she said quietly, and reached down to pick up her coat before walking away.

Chapter Fifteen

There was no work she could do, no projects she could use to occupy her time. All Hannah managed to do when she got home was change into her pajamas and lie on the couch in the living room until David came down to sit beside her.

"Goodnight, Aunt Hannah," he said, wrapping an arm around her when she sat up.

Resting her head on his shoulder, she tried to find some words to comfort him even though it was obvious he could tell she was the one who needed comforting. "I know you were looking forward to your dad coming home for the holidays. I'm sorry that's not going to happen."

Hannah had missed Thomas's call while she'd been at the museum with Elliot, but as she'd driven back to her place, she'd seen the text message he'd left. He wasn't going to make it home in time for the wedding. Michelle must be crushed. Sort of like Hannah was at the moment.

"It's okay, he called and we talked. Some things are out of our control. Are you okay, though?"

He sounded so adult, but she was supposed to be the one keeping an eye on him. She nodded. "Yes. I'm fine."

"If it's any consolation, I think everything's going to be okay."

He had no idea how much those words meant to her, even though Hannah was fairly certain David actually had no idea what had happened between her and Elliot. She certainly hadn't told him anything. Then again, kids had a way of knowing things that adults didn't want them to know. Elliot had once told her that he knew his parents were going to break up before his mother had ever started packing.

She sighed with how sad she'd always thought that was. Her parents had been in her life, together, loving each other, until Hannah was an adult. She could never imagine how Elliot had felt growing up in a home with a different setup. Perhaps that was why he'd handled things the way he had with her. Or maybe it was why he felt the need to search for more. She had no idea, and truthfully, she was tired of thinking about it.

"Goodnight, Auntie," David repeated.

Hannah smiled at her nephew, so grateful that he was there. "Goodnight, David."

When he left her alone again and Hannah lay back on the couch, "The First Noel" began playing from the playlist she'd pulled up on her phone. As she listened, she thought back to all the times she and Elliot had shared together. Even though she'd just told herself she was tired of thinking about it, the memories wouldn't stop replaying.

There was the night they were working late at the Tinker Shop last year trying desperately to fix the snow globe. Their hands had touched and she'd known right then that something was different between them. Her mind circled to the first time they hugged, the kiss at the Christmas festival, how it felt to sit at a piano playing and singing a song with him. Her heart ached in a way she'd never thought possible, but eventually she fell into a fitful sleep.

Six blocks away from the museum, Elliot sat alone in his apartment. The lights on his Christmas tree were set to a timer and were already on when he walked in. He didn't bother to turn on any other lights, just removed his coat and scarf, dropping them both on the couch as he made his way to the rocking chair he kept facing the double windows in the living room.

It had been his mother's chair, and a long time ago it'd sat on the porch of their two-bedroom house. Maggie Lee had loved that little white house on the corner of Rosebud Lane. The rocking chair had taken up most of the space on the tiny porch, but that hadn't stopped her from sitting there every Saturday morning with her cup of coffee in hand. She'd rock for what seemed like hours, long after her coffee was finished, just staring out at the passersby on the street. Someone would come by and she'd lift her hand to wave. If it was Ms. Eleanor from next door, they'd talk for a while about so many things, but mostly about nothing. All the while Elliot would have his bowl of cereal in front of the television in the living room. The morning cartoons keeping him company while the sound of his mother's happy voice gave him a sense of comfort.

Tonight, there was no comfort, not that Elliot could imagine. He dropped his hands to his thighs as he set the chair to rocking. Through the window he could see the Town Square in the distance, so many multicolored lights twinkling with glee. The bell tower on the church stood prominently, just as the gabled roof of City Hall gave a classic feel to the scene. But Elliot closed his eyes to the familiar sight and let his head fall back to rest against the chair.

The scene at the museum instantly replayed in his mind. Hannah's words, "Maybe we should spend some time apart," echoed in his mind. He'd wanted to go to her then, wrap his arms around her and beg her to change her mind. But she'd stepped back and he'd known instinctively to stand still and then back away. She'd never not wanted him to touch her before, had never looked at him with so much sorrow and pain in her eyes as she had tonight. He struggled to figure out what he was supposed to do with the guilt and hurt that filled him because of that.

Remorse bubbled up to the surface next and he clenched his fingers into fists. He'd been nursing the dream of happy ever after with Hannah for so long. It felt like there'd never been another thought for him, another woman, who would complete him. A woman he could love and cherish and share a family with, alongside all his hopes and dreams. For him, it was only her. And for Hannah, it was always going to be Evergreen.

He'd wanted to tell her that it wasn't that he didn't love Evergreen. That couldn't be further from the truth. His mother had brought him here and she'd grown to love this town and there was a part of Elliot that loved it too. But there was a bigger part of him that wanted more. The part that he'd watched die inside his mother each day she was away from the restaurant she'd helped his father build. From the life that she'd made and was happy in, but had left because things with his father hadn't worked out. Elliot desperately wanted to see if that life—the one he'd been forced to leave—had something to offer him now. And he wanted Hannah by his side.

When his phone rang, he sat up in the chair but didn't immediately move to answer it. There was always something interrupting him and Hannah. It'd been that way for as long as he could remember. Except tonight they'd finally found a moment to have the conversation he'd been dreading all along. Hadn't that been why he'd procrastinated telling her about his business plan? Because some part of him had known she'd choose Evergreen over him?

The phone continued to buzz and he squeezed the bridge of his nose, trying to refocus his thoughts, to get a grip on his emotions. It wasn't working, and the phone hadn't stopped ringing. With an exasperated sigh, he reached into his pocket and saw on the screen that it was the representative from the foundation that had given him the loan. He answered the call.

"Hi. Yes, it's good to hear from you too." The words slipped from his mouth, easing around the lump that had formed in his throat after his thoughts of Hannah. "Sure, we can discuss the specifics of the project."

Because there was no use sitting in the dark thinking about something that wasn't going to change. Elliot was always going to love Hannah Turner; unfortunately, that love was no competition for this town.

In the morning, Hannah was still asleep on the couch when David came down to shake her awake.

"Mornin', Aunt Hannah. I fixed you some breakfast," he told her.

Oh, how she loved this intuitive teenager. If she ever had a son, she'd want him to be just like David. The thought came with a burst of sadness, but before it could take over, Hannah forced herself to take a couple bites of the muffin he'd brought, and then carried the cup of coffee upstairs to drink after she'd showered and dressed.

Forty-five minutes later, she stepped out onto the front porch with her coat on and bag on her shoulder. But when she looked out at the dreary day, she saw the light flurries of snow and was reminded of the first snowball fight she and Elliot had together, and of the one they'd had just a couple days ago in front of the Cooper sisters' farm. Bittersweet was the feeling that gripped her tightly.

David came up beside her. "You forgot these," he said, and handed over her red and green mittens. They walked to the Kringle because David had a morning shift today.

"I'll see you at dinner tonight, okay?" Hannah said when they arrived, before he headed back to the kitchen.

"Okay," David told her, and was about to walk away, when Elliot appeared.

He looked as if he was on his way out, with his black coat buttoned and plaid scarf around his neck. He never tied his scarf so that it actually protected him from the cold wind. She fought the urge to tie it for him now.

"Hey," she said after David left them alone. It was too awkward and a bit childish not to say anything, but she'd definitely considered it.

"Hey," he replied.

"Hannah, over here!" Sonya called to her from a table across the room, and Hannah told herself to buy her a gift for that save later.

Without another word, Hannah walked around Elliot, waving at Sonya and finding the smile that her friends were so used to seeing from her.

"Hi," she said approaching the table. "You must be Bea and Gordon. I'm Hannah, Thomas's sister."

Michelle had sent Hannah a text about her father and his new girlfriend finally arriving. The text had been filled with dancing emojis, and Hannah had been excited that Michelle had found at least a little bit of happiness during this very trying time.

"Oh, it's so nice to meet you," Bea said.

"You, too. I heard about the wedding postpone-ment." Just one more spot of bad news to add to a growing list. She kept her smile in place, refusing to let it get her down. "On the bright side, though, we have the Christmas Festival coming up. We have the museum opening, and I can personally guarantee that it's gonna be the—"

"Whoa," Gordon said, with the same hesitant ex-pression she'd seen on Sonya's face. "I'm not sure we're sticking around that long."

"Christmas has never exactly been our thing," Sonya added.

Again, Sonya's voice seemed to carry throughout the restaurant and other patrons around them stopped everything they were doing to stare at her. Hannah was just as shocked at Sonya's words as they were.

"I wouldn't say that too loudly here," she whispered to Sonya, and winked.

"Okay. Okay," Sonya agreed.

Before Hannah could continue with her rundown of fun things to do in town, Michelle and Henry arrived.

"Oh, hey, there you guys are," Michelle said, walking toward the table. "I just had the best idea. So, you know how we were supposed to have our rehearsal dinner at Henry's barn tonight." She looked around the table. "Okay, and everybody knows we had to postpone ev-erything. Well, what if we just have the party anyway?"

Sonya looked skeptical, but Hannah could already see that Michelle was very into this idea. The red coat and dress she wore today looked very festive, and Hannah wondered if it was helping Michelle keep such a positive attitude. Perhaps she should've tried that instead of putting on her puffy gray coat and the gloves that continued to remind her of snowfights with Elliot.

"We have all this food—we can't let it go to waste. And there's all that very expensive Christmas wine we ordered," Michelle continued.

Bea began nodding and Sonya followed, but Gordon was still looking as if he might be holding out. Hannah had already decided it was a good idea, but she wasn't the one Michelle was trying to convince.

"And we can help out, Hannah," Michelle continued, shifting her attention to Hannah. "You need decorations for the Christmas Festival and also for the museum opening."

"Yup," Hannah chimed in, happy to officially be on board with what was obviously making Michelle very happy. "It couldn't hurt."

But Michelle wasn't finished with her pitch. "And Dad, I have wanted you to see this town in all its Christmas glory for the longest time. Right? I've been trying to get you guys to come here."

Gordon chuckled. "Sweetie, now hold on."

Sonya stopped him from whatever he was going to say by putting a hand over his and adding, "You just tell us what to wear and what time."

"Okay, great," Michelle said with a relieved sigh. "Now I need some coffee."

Sonya shook her head. "That is untrue. Let's get you some uncaffeinated cider," she said, and pushed her mug across the table to where Michelle was now sitting.

Happy that at least someone seemed to be making their bad news into something good, Hannah prepared to leave. "So lovely to meet you two."

With that she waved to everyone at the table and headed to the door. She was thinking that Michelle and Thomas were the epitome of love—here they were faced with a snowstorm that was keeping them separated on their wedding day, and yet Michelle was able to smile and see the bright side. That's what love was all about, compromise and sticking together. Oh, what did she know about love? It was obvious she wasn't doing too well in that arena.

Trying not to frown, she kept walking, but came to an abrupt stop when she saw Jeb Cooper sitting at a table alone. He was writing on a pad stuck to a clipboard on one side of the table, with a plate of half-eaten toast and a mug on the other. She should just keep on walking and leave him to scribbling on that paper and mulling over whatever was bothering him today. Except she didn't like seeing anyone so obviously unhappy, especially now that she knew a little bit more about him. Besides, it was Christmas, the time for joy and happiness to prevail, even if it wasn't going to work out that way in her personal life.

She stopped at his table and waited for him to look up. When he did, she waved, which only made him deepen his scowl.

"So," she continued anyway. "There's gonna be a party for Michelle at Henry's farm tonight if you'd like to come," she said.

The lines on his forehead deepened. "Ms. Turner, being overly nice is not going to get you anywhere," he replied.

Well, she could certainly hope. "The council is going through your requests and agreeing to a lot of them."

He continued to give her an impassive stare. Hannah had always been tenacious, so she simply pressed on. He didn't have to like her or what she was doing with the museum, but he could still hear, so she was going to say her piece and then be on her way.

"As for me, I'm grateful that you're allowing us to continue to work at the museum, so thank you for that." He didn't respond and she was about to leave, but paused again. "And, for the record, I read a lot of the articles on the old Hat Factory and I think you did the best you could."

He huffed. "If that were true, the Hat Factory would still be in business and Evergreen would still have an industry."

Jeb looked completely broken by what he'd just admitted to her, and Hannah couldn't help but be reminded of seeing him in that storeroom looking at all those hats last night. He seemed bereft—no, not exactly. It was more like he was lost. As if he'd once known who and what he was and now he didn't. A part of her ached for him in that regard, since she'd been struggling lately with who she was and her place in this town.

"Well, the offer stands," she said. "We'll be going to Miller's farm later, if you'd like to join us."

"No. Thank you," Jeb replied swiftly, and went back to focusing on whatever he was writing.

Hannah, on the other hand, shrugged and continued out of the restaurant. *Nothing beats a failure but a try.* Her mother used to say that. And, for the record, Hannah had just tried with Jeb Cooper, again. If there was any getting through to the guy, someone else would have to do it. For now, Hannah had other things on her schedule to get done, which left no more time to worry over things she just couldn't change.

Michelle had just put on her coat as she stepped outside of the Kringle after having coffee with her father and Bea. Sonya had left with her and now stood beside her on the sidewalk.

"Hi, how are you? Good to see you. How's the family?" Michelle asked a father and son walking down the street.

"Okay," Sonya said after the man had responded and walked on by. "You're up here like twelve ladies piping and I need you down here around four hens a…birding."

On any other day, listening to her sister struggle through one of her favorite songs would've bothered Michelle. Today, she simply corrected her, "Twelve drummers drumming and four calling birds."

"The point is, you certainly seem a little…" Sonya tilted her head with that skeptical look she had patented.

"Well, okay," Michelle said, cutting off whatever else Sonya was going to say. She knew exactly what her sister was thinking and figured she'd just go ahead and address it and get it over with. "Is this the result of being in an un-ideal situation? Maybe. But Thomas is the man of my dreams. I don't mind moving the wedding to Christmas. Shoot, I'd marry that man in July."

And she'd cried enough about the situation. There was nothing else she could do, and staying cooped up in her house moping around about it wasn't the answer.

Sonya chuckled. "All right, I get it. But is the lady perhaps protesting too much?"

Michelle shook her head. "I thought about it. There're upsides. I don't have to plan anymore. I just have to change the date. Pressure's off."

Her sister shrugged, but didn't look totally convinced. "As long as you're sure you're okay."

"I'm fine," Michelle said, taking Sonya's hand for a quick squeeze. "But I think we should've asked Hannah how things were going with Elliot. He was out at Henry's this morning when I got there, talking to Ezra about things he needed to get ready to leave for Boston."

"Hmmm." Sonya shook her head. "So he's still going. Well, she's doing the right thing by staying here and following her own path."

"Maybe," Michelle said. "But I know it hurts. They're so in love. I know how that feels."

"Oh, please, all this love and Christmas cheer is for those calling birds you were just talking about." Sonya sounded like she was over it.

But Michelle knew better. "Don't act like I didn't notice how you and Henry are passing these looks each time you're around each other. You stick around Ever-green long enough and we might be having a double sister wedding come next year."

Sonya shook her head adamantly. "Okay, well, with that ridiculous suggestion, we should be going. Shall we?" Sonya nodded toward the red truck parked beside them.

"We shall," Michelle responded with a smile and watched her sister walk around to the passenger side.

At the church, Carol directed the choir in singing "God Rest Ye Merry, Gentlemen."

It felt different, being in this position. Standing in front of the choir making sure the sopranos hit their notes and the altos and tenors were in perfect harmony. The sound of them all blending in to sing a favorite Christmas song warmed her heart. And convinced her that she was going to be just fine in this position.

When Hannah had first asked her to take over the choir, she'd been hesitant. Not because she didn't love music and enjoy the choir immensely, but more because writing the Kringle cookbook had been her step-out-of-the-box moment. Taking another step into a different arena, so soon, was new to her. Of course, most of the time Hannah made multitasking look easy, if not exhausting.

With that thought she smiled and turned her full attention back to the choir and her new assignment.

"Oh, just so good," she told them. "Excellent work,

everybody! Great rehearsal." Carol took a breath, trying to contain her excitement. "I just want to say thank you so much for welcoming me in. And now, before we go, I wanted to pitch everyone an idea."

Jenny stepped out of the choir stand to lift a white sheet off the table that had been set up there. Under it, the hand bells had been polished and shone brightly lined up on the table.

"Well, I just figured that since we all know how to read music, how hard would it be to learn how to play a little, too?"

Jenny picked up two bells, shaking them until they rang in harmony.

"Are we not going to sing all the carols?" David asked.

"Oh no, we absolutely are," Carol replied. "But I just thought that maybe we could—"

"Let's jump right in and try something new and fun!" Josie said.

"A Christmas treat for all of us," Jenny added, still holding the two bells.

Deciding the sisters had finished out her pitch just fine, Carol shrugged. "Well, who's in?"

Unsurprisingly, the Cooper sisters were the first to raise their hands while the other choir members looked around at each other.

Oh, yay, David's hand inched up slowly. Carol almost clapped with glee to have the younger choir member on board. Then Nick raised his hand, and before long, all the hands were up and Carol could feel herself beaming.

Chapter Sixteen

$\mathcal{H}$annah entered the Miller Barn behind Michelle, Gordon, Bea, and Sonya. Carol and Joe had been coming up the path from the opposite direction, so they all walked through the wide front opening together. For a moment Hannah could only stop and stare.

There really was nothing like an Evergreen celebration. Whatever they did there was always top-notch and slightly over the top. This evening was no different. Once again, the barn had been transformed into a Christmas haven, with hundreds of strings of lights stretched from one rafter to the other until they lined the ceiling. Around each post red and green ribbons hugged the wood, giving it a festive glow. Wreaths were hung at measured intervals all around the walls, and of course there were Christmas trees. Too many for Hannah to count while standing here. Six-foot-long tables had been lined in rows to Michelle's specifications. They were covered in white linen with red runners, and instead of being set with plates, cutlery and glasses for the rehearsal dinner, they now had all sorts of craft items and food on top of them, and were surrounded by chattering people.

Inhaling deeply, Hannah took in the sights while letting the fresh crisp winter air refresh her mind. Just as she'd been thinking earlier today when she'd spoken to Jeb Cooper at the Kringle, Christmas was the time of year for joy and happiness. And since they did Christmas so well in Evergreen, there was no way she could not get into the spirit, no matter what else was going on.

"Decoration stations, comfort food, David made eggnog," Joe announced when they still stood in the doorway.

"It's perfect," Michelle said, looking around. "Dad, you have to try the eggnog. David's becoming a master at making it. Oh! And here, I got you one of Hannah's scarves!"

Hannah grinned as Gordon put his hands up to stop the knitted green, red and white scarf from being put around his neck. "Thank you, honey, I appreciate it. But I'll wear it later."

They all laughed and Michelle tucked the scarf into her bag. Hannah enjoyed seeing Michelle so happy that her family was here. Watching her with Gordon reminded Hannah of her father, but they were happy memories and so she continued to smile.

After a few moments, Hannah and Carol broke away from the group, walking around, speaking to people and stopping at some of the different tables.

They settled at a table where there were lots of craft items to make centerpieces. Hannah knew that was the objective of the table from eyeing the long crystal bowl filled with pinecones and sprigs of holly berries. The bowl was surrounded by fresh pine branches with a card sticking out of one end that read, "Make your own!".

"This is a good chance for us to do some decorations for the Christmas Festival," she told Carol after they'd both started on a project.

She looked around the room at the many people milling around, then picked up another bulb and eased it into the jar she was randomly filling with color. Carol had grabbed a wooden box and was using red and gold netting to make a nest inside.

"What's going on?" Carol asked out of nowhere. "And don't tell me 'Nothing' because I know you too well."

Carol did know her as well as anyone in this town, considering how close to her mother she'd been. But Hannah didn't want to stand here in the middle of Michelle's party talking about her breakup with Elliot. Especially since she knew this party was meant to keep Michelle from feeling so bad about her postponed wedding.

"You know," she started, and glanced over to the punch table where Elliot stood talking to Gordon and Joe.

Carol's gaze had followed Hannah's. She nodded and then turned to Hannah. "Is this about Elliot going to Boston? You two didn't work that out?"

Hannah shook her head. "There's nothing to work out. He has his thing and I have mine. It's as simple as that." Those words may've been easy to say but there was nothing simple about what was going on between her and Elliot. "Hey, do you mind if we talk about this later?"

The way Carol's eyes narrowed had Hannah thinking she was going to continue to press the issue, but she didn't. Instead, she put a hand on Hannah's shoulder and gave a little squeeze. "Sure," she said with a slow smile.

Sonya walked up to the table and picked up a sprig of pine, then dropped it as if it were something hot or disgusting.

"So, Sonya," Hannah said, turning her attention toward her. "Any good at centerpiece or wreath-making?"

"Nope," Sonya readily replied. "I'm not. But it's never stopped me before." She tried another piece of pine and smiled good-naturedly.

Moments later Michelle came over to the table and took a seat.

"Michelle, how're you holding up?" Carol asked.

Michelle opened her mouth to respond—a mayor's ready response, Hannah suspected. But then she faltered, her face crumpling until she put her hands up to cover it. Fighting her own sadness, Hannah hurried over to Michelle's side.

"No. No. No. No. No," Hannah said, when she was close to her.

Sonya stepped closer to Michelle's other side, while Carol looked on with concern.

"I mean, I…it's sinking in now," Michelle said. "I drove you guys wedding-crazy for an entire year and now, will anyone even want to come next year?"

"Of course we're all gonna show up," Hannah told her. "All of this was out of anybody's control."

Carol had come to wrap her arms around Michelle now. "We're gonna show up 'cause that's what we do."

Hannah, Carol and Sonya all leaned into Michelle for a group hug. Although the hug was meant to comfort Michelle, it was exactly what Hannah needed as well. The feeling of family, of people who had each other's back no matter what, was exactly what kept her grounded in Evergreen. No way she could ever leave this, not even for the love of her life.

As if somebody knew the mood desperately needed to be shifted, a flurry of snowballs came flying through the open barn doors and hit the table. The four of them startled as a snowball disrupted a pile of holly sprigs and pine cones. Michelle reacted first, shaking her head as she picked up one of the snowballs that had landed on the table.

"Oh no," she said playfully. "Not on Madam Mayor's watch." She stood and hurled it right back outside toward David and Zoe, who were the culprits.

Michelle rushed outside, grabbing handfuls of snow, laughing as she tossed them into the air. Hannah watched as she tossed a snowball at David and he ducked to avoided getting smacked by it. But David was fast; he hurriedly packed another snowball and hurled it toward Michelle. Evergreen's esteemed mayor shouted and ran for cover.

Well, this wasn't how Hannah had thought this party

was going to go, but she was always down for a good snowball fight. With a chuckle, she ran outside too, along with just about everyone who'd been inside the barn. She picked up some snow and glanced around to see Nick standing by the tractor laughing. A snowball thrown by Josie Cooper hit him in the belly and he chuckled some more.

Hannah threw a snowball at Zoe, but the girl was a moving target, and when she turned to aim another one, she caught sight of Sonya and Henry, who weren't participating in the fight, but were standing close, observing and laughing.

Looking around, Hannah could see it was a full-out town-wide snowball fight, and she laughed with how much fun she was having. Carol and Joe were near the stacks of hay, throwing handfuls of unpacked snow that really weren't hitting anybody, but they were laughing and enjoying themselves too.

All of sudden Hannah began getting hit by multiple snowballs from so many different directions she didn't have a chance to stop and make one to toss in retaliation. Making a run for it, she ran over to a table she saw turned on its side and ducked behind it. Seconds later Elliot appeared, using the same safe haven she'd selected.

He looked over at her and they both grinned. Now this felt familiar. She and Elliot together again...in the throes of a snowball fight, that is. The memories combined with the enthusiastic energy of the moment kept her still, her gaze fixed on him.

"They've got us cornered," he said, giving her a knowing glance.

After a nod that said she was thinking the same thing he was, she watched as a slow smile began to spread across his face. They waited a beat before raising up to peek over the rim of the table.

A number of snowballs soared over their heads and they ducked again, then ran toward the trees.

"Oh, they're really asking for it now," she said, reaching down to grab some snow. "They have us pinned down," she added, when they were both squatting behind two trees.

"That's okay," he replied with a wide grin. "We've always been masters at this."

That was so true. She and Elliot had mastered so many things together. Snowball fights was just one of the top five.

"Mittens!" Elliot began looking down at her hands. "You pack with—"

With a nod Hannah finished his statement. "Pack with mittens, but throw..." She offered him the snow.

"Throw with bare hands," he completed what she'd told him years ago, and took the snow from her mitten-covered hand. "Right!" he yelled, before tossing the snowball.

They successfully bombed the duo of Zoe and David, and laughed so hard to celebrate their success that they turned around and bumped right into each other. His arms instantly went around her, to hold Hannah upright, she thought, not to hug her, because they weren't together anymore. But it still felt good, it felt right. How was that even possible?

They were so right together, but destined to be apart. She'd told Elliot she didn't want him to regret not going through with his plan. That was the equivalent of sending him off to Boston with a pat on the back. The thought made fresh hurt shoot through her chest, even while being this close to him. The pain mingled with the love, twisting in the pit of her stomach until she didn't know if she should wrap her arms around him in a real embrace, or turn and run as fast as she could to keep from totally falling apart.

There was nothing left to do. She'd said what she had to say and Elliot had done the same. The reality was that it was over for them. The love she'd waited so long for would soon go away, just as the snow did each year. The revelation was almost unbearable, as the awkwardness between them stretched on a few seconds longer.

Elliot moved first, dropping his arms to his sides. Hannah took a step back, clearing her throat.

"I should probably head back to the museum," she said. "And get those stories together."

"And I should probably get those wreaths packed," he added, his words tumbling over hers.

They both walked away without looking back.

Later that day, Hannah and David sat in the movie room at the museum watching all the completed stories she'd edited together to run on a loop.

"Just our Evergreen story?" Carol asked from the screen.

Hannah recalled she'd answered, "Whatever you love best about it." But that had been edited out of the final version.

"Well, we were both born in Evergreen and we were high school sweethearts," Carol continued, while Joe held her hand.

The scene faded from Joe and Carol kissing to Meg standing at the front desk at the Inn. "So it worked out," her words picked up seamlessly where Joe's had left off. "The more I've been at the Inn, the more I've seen people—"

Footage of Carol teaching the choir to play hand bells, but it not going too well, came alive on the screen next, and Hannah giggled. She'd absolutely done the right thing by asking Carol to take over directing the choir.

"People find each other," Ezra's voice sounded when he appeared on screen. "And no matter how it works out or even if it doesn't, love leads us to—"

Listening to Ezra brought on a fresh pang of sadness that Hannah fought hard to stifle. He'd moved away from Evergreen to build on a relationship and had been unlucky in love too. Shaking her head, she pushed that memory aside just as Michelle appeared on screen. She was at the Kringle with Mr. Cooper, once again going over his list of demands. Hannah prayed daily that the mayor would be able to talk some sense into the stubborn man.

"To places like Evergreen, where love is liable to turn up where you least expect it, or—" Nick's voice trailed off and Hannah sat up straighter as she watched the next scene.

It was Elliot painting the Evergreen mural in the Tinker Shop, and her adding details to the entryway of the museum. Going about their daily lives, she thought as she watched. Doing the things they loved. Or so Hannah had thought. To be fair, maybe Elliot did love what he was doing in Evergreen, but he also needed to do something else. She could understand that, couldn't she?

The video continued with Allie and Zoe sitting in chairs.

"Or, right where you left it. Love isn't just about a person. It can be about a place."

Allie smiled at Zoe. A mother and daughter. It was a sweet scene and one that again had Hannah's emotions bubbling over. Would she have a family now? Did she need to head over to the Kringle to make yet another wish on the snow globe?

Hannah pushed pause on the movie because her heart was swelling with sentiment. Everyone on this screen was her family and Evergreen was her home, of that there had never been any doubt. So why did she still feel so awful about not wanting to go with Elliot, the man she loved with all her heart? Was there a way to have it all—for him to follow his dreams and her to fulfill her purpose?

This wasn't the time to go deeply into thought about that, or break down with the intensity of it all; she had work to do. Hannah pressed play again and cleared her throat as the Cooper sisters appeared on screen next.

She smiled at the sight of them, loving how close they were—and not just because they were twins, but because they genuinely liked each other. They were also a joy to be around, always with a kind word or a funny observation.

"By the time we found out that the factory was out of money and was going to close," Josie said. On screen Josie handed Hannah the newspaper clipping the night they were taping the story and Hannah read it. So when she'd seen Jeb at the Kringle this morning, she'd told him she knew what happened to the Hat Factory.

"It was too late. The news had hit the stands," Jenny continued.

"Poor Jeb really took the weight of it on himself," Josie said. "He never was one to ask for help—his pride gets in the way."

Jenny nodded. "I think he didn't want to run a factory, he wanted to uphold our family legacy. And he tried."

"One last question," Hannah could hear herself say in the video. "What does the Hat Factory mean to you both?"

Josie and Jenny looked at each other, puzzled, and the video faded out.

Hannah picked up the remote and turned the video off. She was sitting on one of the antique couches that had been found in the warehouse and cleaned until the gold arms and legs gleamed. The plush red backing and seat cushion were ornate and reminded Hannah of a throne fit for royalty. David sat across from her in another chair that had been restored.

"So Mr. Cooper feels like he failed the town, which I guess I understand," she began. "This building turning into something else is really hard for him." She tried to put herself in his position, to think of how she'd feel if the Tinker Shop was being turned into something else. But isn't that exactly what she and Elliot had already begun doing with the shop? They'd transformed it into a multipurpose space that the town loved and that would soon have a second location.

"So, surprise him," David replied, and then came to sit next to her on the couch. "See, I want Michelle and my dad to know that I think about them, so I decided to surprise them with a song at their wedding."

Hannah didn't dare tell him that she knew he was taking those piano lessons for his dad. Instead, she smiled, touching a hand to her heart at his words. When had her charming little nephew grown into such a considerate young adult?

"Which I guess now I'll have to save for another time. But—"

"But you feel we need to show Mr. Cooper that we appreciate him," Hannah continued, following David's train of thought.

David shrugged and reached for his red hat and put it on.

"Hat," Hannah said, watching David turn to her and adjust the hat. The idea came so suddenly and clearly she couldn't help but grin.

"What?" David asked.

"Nothing," she said in response to his alarm, and touched a hand to his shoulder. "I think I've found a solution to my Mr. Cooper problem."

With a sigh of relief she leaned in and hugged her nephew, who was still looking very confused. "I gotta get to work." She didn't wait for another reply from David, but instead jumped up and ran out of the movie room.

Giddy with the excitement that always came to her with a fresh idea, she made her way down the long corridors of the museum, passing the many exhibits that were already completed. Her booted feet clicked across the floor when she saw her destination just ahead.

Coming to the room where she'd seen Mr. Cooper the other day, Hannah opened the door and stared inside. Her heart thumped wildly after the exertion of moving so fast to get here, but she couldn't help it; her smile continued to spread as she looked at what was inside. There were round hat boxes and regular square boxes and so many hats sitting on top of the boxes, stacked and propped against the wall. With a grin she rubbed her hands together, knowing exactly what she was going to do to show Mr. Cooper how much they appreciated all he'd done for the town.

Hannah made one last detour that night, heading over to the Tinker Shop. *It's not to see Elliot*, she told herself. They'd talked about things and decided how they were going to proceed. There was nothing more to be said, although she was certain there were still so many unresolved feelings for them both.

"Hey, I was just popping by to check up and see how the painting—" She paused when she saw it behind him. Finished.

There were no words, or if they were, they didn't come easily as she walked closer, her gaze focused on the painting. Elliot had gotten everything just right. From the snow on the ground to the couple walking across the street with their tiny puppy. The huge Christmas tree in the center of the Town Square lit up in all its majestic glory, and the infamous red truck that had belonged to Allie's grandfather. The painting looked exactly like the mural her parents had painted so many years ago. Their picture, the one of them standing proudly smiling hand in hand in front of the mural, was clipped to the side of the painting.

Love, adoration, gratitude and pride swelled in her chest. "Oh, Elliot."

When she momentarily tore her gaze away from the portrait to glance at him, he was cleaning his paint brush while staring at the painting. The look on his face as he surveyed his work was of pure reverence. The set of his lips and the intense focus of his eyes spoke of nothing but love and respect for the original artists of this piece. And every stroke of his brush had paid homage to them. Hannah's heart was so full she could barely speak.

Instead she turned her attention to the painting once more, moving once again toward the easel that held the painting.

"I won't lie," he said, his tone thoughtful. "It was, um, strange being here without you. But I get it, you're busy."

"Thomas always said I got that from our parents." She remained still, staring at the painting, a sense of melancholy blanketing her. "I guess keeping busy was my way of touching all the things they touched. But this...this is like having them back for Christmas." She turned to face him. "Thank you."

"You continue their legacy. The museum will do that. But you can ask...you don't have to run yourself ragged doing it."

"Right," she said, wistfully accepting the advice from a friend. Was she ever going to get used to this new phase of their relationship? They'd always been friends, but being in love had changed that, and now they were just friends again. It all seemed so surreal, and yet so permanent.

Unable to change what was, Hannah moved, intending to get out of his way, but instead she ended up right in front of him. They stared at each other awkwardly—something else that was becoming the new reality for them.

"Excuse me," she said. "I've just gotta grab my camera equipment." That was another reason she'd stopped by the Tinker Shop. There always seemed to be a reason she needed to be there, and she wondered if that would change once Elliot was gone.

He moved out of her way. "Right."

She hurried behind the counter to grab her camera bag, telling herself this would get easier. That in a while she'd be so busy with the museum that she wouldn't feel every sharp slice of agony at not being with Elliot. But for now, she needed to get out of here, to put some space between them and give her tumultuous emotions a chance to calm down. She put the bag on her shoulder and circled the counter again, this time heading for the door.

Elliot stepped in front of her, blocking the path. "Would you like to go with me to Michelle and Thomas's wedding?" His question came out of nowhere. They hadn't talked about Michelle and Thomas or anyone else in the few times they'd seen each other since last night, and it was odd that he'd bring it up now.

"Oh," was all she could manage to say. It also hadn't occurred to her that he'd even want to return to Evergreen for her brother's wedding.

"When it does happen, whatever we are then, I'd like to go with you," he continued. "It's a special day for your family, so it's a special day for me." Because she was his family, Hannah thought. He didn't say that part, but he'd said it to her before. He'd told her that she, Thomas and her parents had filled an emptiness in him that he'd lost when his parents had divorced.

She wondered if he'd feel empty again once he moved to Boston. Would he miss the family he'd become such an integral part of in Evergreen? Or the friends? Or her?

"Then yes," she said, before clearing her throat. "I'd love to." There was no sense in denying the truth.

Elliot's smile came quickly, sending an unexpected blast of hope through her. It was a familiar warm smile that had her stepping closer to him. How was she going to survive not seeing that smile every day?

Her question went unanswered, as the bells above the door jingled. Hannah looked over Elliot's shoulder to see David and Sonya walk in.

"So, do you think we can pull it off?" David asked Sonya.

Elliot had turned to face them now as well, but looked over his shoulder to give Hannah a quizzical look. She shared his unspoken sentiment as she wondered what David and Sonya were talking about as well.

"And what kind of auntie would I be if I said no?" Sonya answered his question with a question...and a smile. "Let's ask Aunt Hannah."

Oh no, it was something for the "aunties." Hannah wondered how this was going to play out. And if it would be a welcome distraction from the tension hovering between her and Elliot.

Lifting a brow, she stared at both of them. "Ask Aunt Hannah what?"

Chapter Seventeen

E ven though Hannah was proud of herself for cutting
some of the projects off her list, on the 23rd of December she was still rushing through the Town Square
when Jeb Cooper stepped out in front of her.

"So," he said without any pleasantries. Hannah
managed a smile. "I saw that the town council agreed
to my demand for one third of the admission fees and
gift shop profits."

"Yes, they did," she replied. "So I guess this is it
for us—"

"I still want to make sure the museum is up to my
standards," he interrupted.

It occurred to her that he'd still never told her what
about this project would make him happy. While she understood that losing the business had hurt him immensely, she couldn't help but wonder if he really planned
to go through the rest of his life scowling at people.
It certainly seemed like a waste of life to her, and she
could speak to that with a bit of experience. Her heart
was still breaking over the demise of her relationship

with Elliot, yet she'd gotten out of bed this morning and smiled as she prepared for the day.

Another one of her quick ideas popped into her mind and she said, "Come by tomorrow. I've made something I think might convince you."

For a split second she was rewarded by the look of surprise on his face. But that momentary brightness she'd seen in his eyes quickly faded, and he grumbled, "Hmmm. We'll see."

When he walked away, Hannah released a sigh and muttered, "We'll see," before walking off.

Michelle was sitting on her couch on the evening that was supposed to be her wedding night, lacing popcorn onto string to hang on the tree.

"I've always had a lot of questions about *It's A Wonderful Life*," Sonya said, coming up behind her. "Why does the old man keep so many animals at the bank? There's a squirrel, a crow…"

Michelle shrugged and grinned. Leave it to Sonya to critique a movie. "It's a Christmas movie; there're going to be eccentric characters."

Sonya came around to sit on the couch beside Michelle. "I think I know what might cheer you up." When Michelle only gave her an uninterested look, her sister continued. "Go try on your wedding dress."

Michelle picked up more popcorn and eased it into her mouth. "That is the exact opposite of what would cheer me up, considering this is the night I was supposed to be getting married." Why would Sonya even suggest something like that? It was all Michelle could do not to keep focusing on the fact that she should've been getting married tonight.

"I wanna see it," Sonya whined, the way she used to when they were kids and she didn't get her way. "Come on, do it for me, the maid of honor."

Okay, that almost worked. But Michelle shook her head. "I don't want anyone to see my wedding dress until there's an actual wedding."

Sonya nodded. "That makes sense. But then I insist that we all get dressed up for dinner."

Michelle paused again. Sonya was watching Christmas movies and suggesting a dress-up dinner?

"Come on, it'll make us feel better," Sonya continued to coax her.

Going back and forth with her sister was probably pointless, and besides, Michelle didn't feel like arguing. She felt like sitting on this couch drowning her sorrows in the popcorn she was eating more of than threading and watching *It's A Wonderful Life* for the billionth time. Still, her family was here to visit with her; the least she could do was be hospitable. "Okay," she said, tossing her hands up in defeat.

Sonya smiled. "Thank you."

Still skeptical of this whole idea, Michelle reluctantly got up from the couch and walked upstairs. Once inside her bedroom, she closed the door behind her and leaned against it. What was she doing? How had this happened to her?

For months she'd been planning the perfect small but sentimental wedding to a man she loved with all her heart. Everything was going to be exactly as she and Thomas had envisioned, because she'd been sure to include him in every decision that needed to be made. A smile ghosted across her lips as she thought about how attentive and patient Thomas had been whenever she brought up plans for the wedding.

He'd even selected two of the songs the choir was going to sing, as well as the flavor of the four-tiered cake they'd planned to have. Of course, chocolate cake was her absolute favorite, so there wouldn't have been any argument from her on that front. Chuckling now, she wondered if their guests would've enjoyed the cake. Would they have danced all night to the band that they'd hired to play? Josie and Jenny sure would've—those two loved to dance.

Still hating that her special day had been canceled, but loving that she could at least smile when thinking about it, Michelle moved to her closet.

Let's get dressed up for dinner, she recalled Sonya saying.

"What on earth happened to my sister? Was watching *It's a Wonderful Life* getting to her?" Michelle laughed out loud at that question. Sonya wouldn't have liked her making that assumption.

Sliding a few hangers that held dresses out of her way, Michelle settled on a black gown and wondered if that might be a little too dressy.

"Well, she said 'Let's get dressed up,' so I'm gonna

get dressed up." With that thought, she tossed the dress on her bed and went to her makeup stand.

When her face was done and she'd restyled her curly hair, Michelle put on the dress and headed down the stairs.

"Wow! Well, would you look at that," Sonya said when Michelle once again stood in the living room.

Michelle did a little turn, then stopped to strike a pose. Both she and Sonya laughed at the action, and she admitted to herself that she was feeling a little better.

"Okay, now that you're in that stunning black gown," Sonya said, "I've got a surprise for you."

Watching as Sonya stepped to the side, Michelle was indeed surprised when "The First Noel" began to play. Her gaze rested on David, wearing a blue suit as he sat at the piano, his fingers moving purposefully over the keys.

This was her stepson, the child she'd never imagined having. He was a perfect gift from Thomas and she'd promised herself from the moment she'd said yes to Thomas's proposal that she'd be the very best stepmother she could possibly be to him.

Totally in awe of how well he played, Michelle walked up behind David. When he knew she was standing there, he stopped and looked up at her. After sharing a smile, she sat on the bench beside him.

"Where did you learn how to do this?" Thomas had never mentioned that David could play.

He blushed and something tightened around her heart. "The Cooper sisters taught me," he proudly replied.

"Oh, David, you're so good." If she'd known him all his life Michelle wouldn't have been able to love him more than she did right at this moment. "David, I know it's hard being here without him."

"That's okay," David said, and looked around. "I'm with family. I have Aunt Hannah, Aunt Sonya and I have you. Now, come on, I have another surprise."

David got up and extended his hand to her. He looked so handsome and so much like his dad, her heart swelled with love. She accepted his hand and they walked out into Michelle's backyard.

Michelle's breath caught as they stepped through the open doors. Her patio had been completely transformed, and all she could do was look around with tears quickly forming.

On every bush, hanging from the trim of the house, and draped around the Christmas tree now sitting in the farthest corner from the house were white twinkle lights. Gold candelabras stood on tables covered in white linen cloths. White flowers filled crystal vases, silver bulbs hung from white frosted branches and the Evergreen choir stood dressed in their festive red robes.

Michelle's eyes widened. Where had all of this come from? What was happening? But those questions filtered out of her mind the moment she heard Thomas's voice.

"Thanks for setting up the camera so I could see her, Sis."

"Turner siblings' rules: We always have each other's backs. Right?" Hannah, who wore a burgundy sweater dress, said to him.

"Forever and always," Thomas replied from the big-screen television that had been set up on a table surrounded by two white trees with silver and frosted white bulbs hanging from each branch.

Settling her gaze on the screen, Michelle's heart melted at the sight of her husband-to-be. Thomas wore a dark brown velvet jacket over a crisp white shirt, and he was looking at her as if she were the only woman in the world. Oh, how she wanted to reach out and touch him. To cup her palm against his cheek, or step into his embrace. He would hold her tightly and she'd wish, as she'd done so many times before, that he would never let her go.

"What?" was the only question Michelle she could ask when words finally formed in her mind. Hannah handed her a glass of champagne. She didn't have a clue what was happening or who'd put all this together, but she knew she'd be forever grateful.

Hannah didn't respond, but instead, left Michelle alone with her husband-to-be on the TV screen.

"Wow, you look fabulous," Thomas said as Michelle sat on one of the cushioned deck chairs. "Your family said that you were feeling sad."

Michelle sighed, loving and being annoyed at her family simultaneously.

"Late last night I got a call," Thomas continued, "from David and your sister, and I thought you could use a little love today. So if you don't mind, a sneak peek at my wedding vows."

"Oh, Thomas," was all she could manage to say.

"Your grace and your strength drew me right to you. Instantly. I've watched you with David and I love how our lives just fit. You were the missing piece of this puzzle and I'm so happy to call us family."

When he paused, Michelle took a steadying breath. This man really was everything to her. Hearing him declare them a family was the icing on the cake.

"Michelle, I am humbled to be the man who gets to take your hand one day soon," he said.

She gasped, shaking her head and praying she wouldn't cry. "Thomas, love was an afterthought before you. It wasn't even on my radar. I was just fine with how things were, but loving you has been the easiest, most joyful thing I've ever done in my life. Now we get to be a family and that's all I ever need to know in this world." She let out a huge sigh of relief at how right this moment felt. "I love you."

"And I love you."

At that moment, Carol, Joe and the choir came closer, all of them holding hand bells.

"Tonight is just for you," Thomas told her. "I want you to just relax and enjoy yourself. And I promise I'll be home as soon as I can."

As Michelle blew a kiss at the TV screen that went blank soon after, the choir began to play the bells and sing. Light refreshments courtesy of the Kringle were served on silver trays and more champagne was passed around.

"Happy not wedding day," Sonya said, when Michelle joined her and Hannah near the patio doors.

"Or whatever today is—happy that." Sonya lifted her glass to toast.

A few feet away, Gordon, Bea, David and Elliot stood smiling.

"Thank you all so much," Michelle told them.

"Hey, what are sisters for?" Hannah said with a grin, and touched her glass to theirs for a toast.

Hannah and David walked home later that night, marveling at all the lights and decorations around town as if they'd never seen them before. Tonight had been special and romantic and everything she, Sonya and David had hoped for Michelle to experience. Seeing Thomas and Michelle staring at each other with that loving gaze, knowing that even though this wasn't the night they had planned, it had still turned out to be special, had touched her heart. And made her think of Elliot.

He'd been so handsome wearing black slacks, white turtleneck and a heather gray blazer tonight, smiling and talking to everyone as he always did. The people of Evergreen loved him, and most of them seemed genuinely happy about him opening another Tinker Shop in Boston. Everyone but Hannah. But no, that wasn't correct, she was happy for him. She hadn't lied when she told him his idea was smart. What she hadn't told him was how proud she was that he would be the one carrying on the Turner name in the industry.

They crossed the street and were just passing the church when Hannah heard music coming from the small building. It was after ten in the evening, so there shouldn't be anyone in the church, but the piano playing was proof that there was. And when she let herself really listen to the melody, her heart warmed because she knew the song.

It was "Give Love on Christmas Day," the song Elliot had played at last year's Christmas Festival. Hannah had sat on the bench with him that night, moving her hands as if she were playing, but singing along instead.

"I can walk the rest of the way by myself. It's only two blocks."

Hannah hadn't realized she'd stopped walking until David spoke. Without knowing the words to respond, she nodded and squeezed his hand. Standing there, she watched until he'd crossed another street. Then, she turned toward the church and took a deep breath, letting it out slowly before walking up the front steps. She stepped inside the church, the same way she had so many times before, but tonight, Hannah knew it was different.

The overhead lights were out, leaving the sanctuary illuminated by only the white twinkle lights hung throughout. It seemed warm in the space and much smaller than usual.

When Elliot looked up to see her standing by the door, he gave a little nod for her to join him.

"What are you doing here so late?" she asked, after walking down the aisle and taking a seat on the bench beside him.

She watched his fingers moving over the keys,

waiting until she thought she had picked up the right note, before starting to play along with him.

"I came here to think," he said.

"Well, we've always been good at a duet." It was her attempt at keeping things light, but that was pointless. What was between them now was as heavy as it got.

"An unstoppable pair," he replied, staring at her.

She continued to play along until Elliot stopped, placing a hand over hers. They stared at each other then, no words necessary.

On instinct, Hannah leaned in and touched her lips to his.

Elliot joined in the kiss and she closed her eyes, marveling at how perfect it felt to be with him. Whether they were working at the Tinker Shop, having a snowball fight, or sitting at a piano kissing when they should've been playing, it was always just right.

It was a short kiss, but nonetheless tender and heart-felt.

"That was unexpected," he said when it was over, but he didn't move away.

Regret immediately seized Hannah and she turned away, focusing her gaze on the piano keys once more. "Oh. I shouldn't have done that."

"No, no," Elliot said quickly and touched a hand to hers. "I'm glad you did."

For what seemed like endless moments their gazes held and all Hannah could wonder was if she'd ever feel this way about someone else again. The answer was probably no, and it broke her heart to admit it.

"But I'm also confused," Elliot continued. "I just keep thinking there's gotta be a way to make this work."

She heard his words and wished with everything inside her that there was a way. All the options had run on repeat in her mind these past few days, but the probability of any of them working was slim. At least for her anyway. "We already know what love looks like," she told him. "I want us to be like we were. Seeing each other every day, working together, being with our friends together. We wouldn't be okay with long distance."

"You're right, we wouldn't be." He shook his head. "But what if it turns out that we do want different things? And…what if we were in too deep, and there's no friendship to go back to?"

With a resigned sigh she answered, "If your heart is pulling you elsewhere, a friend won't stand in your way. And certainly not me."

For an instant, Hannah felt hopeful and expectant, the same way she knew they'd both felt together at one time. But she didn't know how to say that, and when his silence stretched on, she gave him a faint smile and touched his hand before standing. She walked out of the church, knowing without a doubt that she was leaving a chunk of her heart back there on the bench with Elliot.

On Christmas Eve morning, Hannah sat at a table in the Kringle, staring off into space, wondering how her new year was going to be without Elliot, when Allie came out of the kitchen.

"Hey. Look alive," Allie said, and tossed the keys in Hannah's direction.

Hannah looked up just in time to catch them. She grinned at her longtime friend who wore jeans and a red blouse today.

Allie stood at the counter and handed a receipt book to her mother who was slicing and boxing pieces of strudel. "So, let's say you don't get this signature from Mr. Cooper. Does he shut down the museum?"

"Oh, he wouldn't," Hannah started to say, and then sat back in her chair. "Oh, I hope not. We've all worked too hard for that." She sighed with that new thought now resting heavily on her mind. "I just need him to see this one last thing that I made. For Michelle. For the reporters who came into town. For myself."

"Little secret," Allie said, as she walked toward the table.

Hannah stood to meet her, pushing her purse up onto her shoulder.

"I have faith in you," Allie continued. "The whole town does. I mean, that's what Evergreen is, right? It's a town that was built on Christmas wishes."

When Allie handed her the jar of hot cocoa, Hannah took it, feeling the warmth of friendship and love circling her.

"And," Carol said as she and David came to stand beside Allie. "If my mom's cherry strudel recipe doesn't help convince Mr. Cooper to sign, I don't know what will."

Hannah accepted the cheery red box that contained

the strudel. It smelled so good she prayed it would do the trick.

"I made it myself," David added.

She couldn't help but beam with pride. "You're just turning into the snack king."

Like a typical teenager he shrugged, but the smile he gave said her words meant a lot to him.

"Thanks, guys," Hannah said, holding the mug and box up. "Wish me luck!"

"Good luck," Carol said.

"We love you," Allie and David added.

Hannah walked away feeling a lot lighter than she had when she'd come into the Kringle, but just as she was about to go out the door, she paused and looked back. The snow globe was there, sitting on the glass-topped counter right next to the antique cash register where it always was.

Hadn't she said she wasn't going to do this again? No, she recalled, she'd asked herself if she should, but then had smartly declined giving a response. Now, she walked back and picked up the snow globe, holding it tight, but gently in both hands this time. She closed her eyes and wished from the very bottom of her heart. After a few seconds she opened her eyes again, looking at the tiny flutters of snow drifting in the liquid-filled globe. A small smile began to spread and this time, after putting the globe back in its place, she did walk out the door into the fresh morning air.

There was a pep in her step now, a measure of faith she hadn't experienced before, pushing her along to do what she knew had to be done. She was so focused on her task that when she turned to walk toward the truck, she bumped right into Nick…again.

They both laughed.

"Sorry, Nick," she said, when they were both steady and could take a step away.

"Let me guess," he said, "you were in a rush."

"And let me guess, I needed a little nudge to slow me down."

"At least this time it wasn't the snow globe shattering." After more chuckling, Nick suddenly sobered and touched a hand to her arm. "Hannah, I say this with all my heart. All your wishes are granted if you just stop and look around."

He didn't wait for Hannah to respond, which was good, because she didn't think she had a response. As cryptic sayings and Nick went hand in hand, she wasn't surprised by his words, but she did stand in the middle of the Town Square wondering at their true meaning for a few seconds. Finally, she climbed into the red truck and drove off.

Chapter Eighteen

"Sonya, I have some last-minute Christmas shopping to do if you'd like to join," Bea said, as they sat at the island in Michelle's kitchen on Christmas Eve.

Bea sat beside Michelle while Sonya was on the other side of the island, clearing the breakfast dishes.

"No, thanks," Sonya said. "I did mine early."

Frowning because she knew better, Michelle shook her head. "Which means she hasn't done any yet."

When Sonya glared at her, Michelle returned the look with a knowing gaze. "Not true," Sonya replied.

"Oh," Bea chimed in. "Well, maybe we can all go into town and look at decorations. Or—"

Sonya held up her hands. "Thanks, Bea. I think the festival is enough Christmas for me."

Michelle didn't like Sonya's curt way of dismissing Bea, and she was certain that Bea could sense Sonya's standoffish demeanor with her.

"She's not like that all the time," Michelle said to Bea, who was looking more than a little hurt after Sonya walked away.

Bea nodded. "I understand. It's not easy accepting someone new into the tight fold you girls and your father have built."

That was true enough, but it didn't quite excuse Sonya's behavior, in Michelle's book. "Not after my mom passed away. It was like we were all each other had, but not enough for us to move back to the same state to be close to each other. If that makes any sense."

Bea chuckled. "It does. I have five sisters and two brothers and none of us lives in the same state. I believe we're better friends because of it."

"I can see that," Michelle said. "But Sonya will come around. She just misses our mother."

"Well, I'm not planning on going anywhere, so I'll be here when she comes around," Bea said, and Michelle couldn't help but like her a little bit more.

A few hours later, Michelle found Sonya in the family room watching television. Her father and Bea were in the kitchen making Gordon's famous collard greens for tomorrow night's Christmas dinner.

"Here you go, sis," Michelle said, handing Sonya a mug of hot chocolate as she sat down beside her.

"No peppermint?" Sonya asked, after accepting the mug and looking down to see what was inside.

"Ha!" Michelle laughed, and held out the peppermint stick she'd been holding in her other hand to drop into the mug. "Now you like it, huh?"

"Mmm hmm." Sonya nodded and smiled brightly

before turning her attention to the TV again.

"Are you watching *It's A Wonderful Life* again?" This was the fourth time she'd seen Sonya absorbed in this movie since she'd been in town.

"It's always on," Sonya said. "I don't understand the choices any of these people make. But somehow it's so soothing."

Well, if anybody needed soothing, it was Sonya. And Michelle loved seeing her so comfortable on the couch, a fluffy blue and white blanket wrapped around her legs, enjoying a Christmas movie, of all things.

She almost hated to start the discussion she knew needed to be had. But after speaking to Bea this morning and realizing how much the woman cared about her father, she had to say something to Sonya.

"Hey, you think we're being too rough on Bea? And by 'we' I mean you."

The frown came first—it was Sonya's signature annoyed look—but then her sister relaxed. "Look, I know I can be...you know me. It's just strange that Daddy's dating, and I know that might sound childish, but I can't help it. I'm not used to seeing him with anyone other than Mom."

Michelle could relate to how her sister was feeling, but she also knew that not liking something wasn't liable to change it. "What did Mom say she always wanted?"

The look Sonya gave her now was filled with softness as the memory of their mother took center stage in her mind. "For all of us to be happy," Sonya said.

Michelle sighed. "Sweet girl, that includes Daddy."

Sonya looked across the room to Michelle's blue, silver and white-decorated Christmas tree. "Mom loved Christmas. It was her thing. It just feels weird to be celebrating without her." She looked toward the kitchen and lowered her voice. "Not to mention with someone new."

"I think what you're saying is that you miss her," Michelle said. "And I miss her too. Christmas *was* her thing. But maybe now it can be *our* thing. A way for us to stay close to Mom but bring our new family together." When Sonya smiled, Michelle touched a hand to her knee and Sonya covered that hand with her own.

"Now, I'm gonna go help Daddy in the kitchen," Michelle told her, and squeezed Sonya's hand.

"Well, I'm gonna sit right here with my peppermint hot cocoa and finish watching this movie."

"You do that." Michelle chuckled as she got up and walked toward the kitchen.

Seconds later, Bea came into the room to sit on the opposite end of the couch from where Sonya was sitting. She held a mug too, but Sonya figured hers might be coffee since it didn't have a peppermint stick on the side.

"I never understood why Jimmy Stewart didn't just leave town," Bea said.

"I have exactly the same question," Sonya replied.

Bea nodded at her. "And can we talk about the fact that there's a crow...indoors?"

She looked aghast and Sonya could totally relate to that. "And a squirrel," she said. "And a monkey."

"In a bank!" Bea added.

Michelle had fixed herself a cup of coffee and stood at the island with her father watching Bea and Sonya chattering on about the movie.

"Your mom would be so proud of you both," Gordon said.

Michelle leaned in closer to her father to rest her head on his shoulder.

Hannah arrived at the museum a little after noon. She walked up to the entrance, loving the way the giant candy canes and lollipops were lined along the exterior of the building as if they were somehow guarding the place. The cheerful snowman by the door, with the huge poinsettia sprig on his top hat, said Christmas and cheer were in the air...even if surly Jeb Cooper was standing right beside it.

Hannah stopped the moment she saw Mr. Cooper turn around and almost bump into someone walking toward the tents and tables that had been set up for the Christmas Festival. He hurriedly moved out of that person's way, but then turned abruptly and almost bumped into another person. This too befuddled the man and Hannah noted his mood was the same as ever. With that in mind, she held the box with the strudel between her hands and closed her eyes to get in one last prayer before she had to meet with him.

"Mr. Cooper," she said seconds later, as she walked up behind him. "It's nice to see you."

He grumbled something when he turned to see her,

then huffed. "So. All this is for the Christmas Festival, is it?"

"Yes, sir," Hannah replied brightly. "You sure you won't stay for it?"

"Ms. Turner, you have my undivided attention. For the next…" He lifted his wrist to look at his watch. "One hour, exactly. Then I must catch my train."

"Well, I will personally drive you to the train station if you decide that you don't like what you see here." Where that confidence had come from, she had no idea, but she decided to roll with it.

Mr. Cooper continued to frown.

"But either way," she said and extended the box of strudel to him. "Merry Christmas."

He hadn't taken the box from her, but when they got inside the museum, she'd set the box down next to the entrance so she'd remember to give it to him again on his way out.

She walked them directly to the gift shop after they entered.

"We thought we'd fill the gift shop with the ornaments made by the Tinker Shop art classes." As she talked, he walked around looking at the many shelves stuffed with every conceivable ornament ever made in the town.

There were red trucks, bells, advent calendars, keys galore, snow globe replicas and snowmen hats.

"Only way to turn a profit," Mr. Cooper said gruffly.

Hannah wanted to clap with his almost imperceptible nod of approval. "Now, if you'll follow me this way, I have a surprise."

He granted her another grimace. "I've never been a fan of surprises."

"Well, I think I've found a way to honor Evergreen's history," Hannah said, while walking ahead of him.

They moved through another hallway filled with displays, including the one with a life-size replica of the front of the Kringle Kitchen. She noticed him checking out each item in the displays. She slowed her stride to allow time for his perusal, and then happily continued on to the back room.

When she stopped in front of a closed door, she looked up at the sign and waited for Mr. Cooper to do the same.

It read, *The Jeb Cooper Room*, but he didn't say that out loud.

He did, however, take off his hat, holding it in front of him with both hands. "What've you done?"

She stepped in front of him and opened the double doors to the newly decorated room. Excitement bubbled in the pit of her stomach as she waited for his reaction. Of course there was a Christmas tree in one corner, decorated in red, silver and white bulbs and ornaments, white lights twinkling brightly. That same color scheme stretched along garlands that hung around the room as a border near the ceiling and wrapped around the legs of tables throughout the space. On the back wall, dozens of hats hung around the picture of Hiram Cooper and a larger frame that explained the history of the Evergreen Hat Factory.

"It's a tribute to the Evergreen Hat Factory," she said, moving inside. "Our first industry. This building is where it all started."

Mr. Cooper followed her inside. "You've created a display," he said, and extended a hand toward the wall of hats, being careful not to touch anything. "About me, my family. And you've humiliated me in the process. Is that what you've decided to do, shame me?"

"No, no." Hannah scrambled to figure out what was happening here. "It's to honor you and the work that your family has done."

"Hiram Cooper built this company with his hard work. And when he passed it down to good people who put their hearts and souls into it, it ended with me," he said vehemently. "This just calls that out."

"No," Hannah insisted. "It's not your fault. Businesses come and go."

"I could've saved it," he told her. "I let everyone down. My family and my sisters." He stopped and huffed, shaking his head. "All right, we're done here. I'm shutting this all down."

He started walking toward the door but Hannah jumped in front of him. "What? No, Mr. Cooper, you can't. It's Christmas Eve; people are counting on us. The Christmas Festival starts in a few hours."

"And I still own this building," he said, putting up a hand to stop her from talking. "And if I want to take it back from the town, I certainly can. I've read the contract. While I may be—"

"Stubborn!" That was enough from him. Hannah

couldn't take it another second. "Look, if the story of this town tells me anything, it's that sometimes people remember things differently than how they actually happened, and that can make it difficult to see the truth and move forward." She only paused briefly, refusing to let him jump in with another argument. "Mr. Cooper, you've been holding on to a past that, frankly, you don't need to anymore. No one in this town holds anything against you."

For a few seconds Jeb Cooper only stared at her, and Hannah thought maybe, just maybe she'd finally gotten through to him. She was woefully wrong.

He stepped closer to her. "The only thing I'm holding on to is my decision not to open the museum."

Hannah was stunned and disappointed. "You wanted to leave your mark on Evergreen. That's all I've ever wanted to. We both can win if we just take a deep breath—"

"Ms. Turner," he said. "We've both failed. So it goes."

With that he walked out the door, leaving Hannah to stare after him in disbelief and fight back the tears that stung her eyes. She only stood there for a few seconds, refusing to let Jeb Cooper take up more of her time or emotions. She'd done all she could do; unfortunately, it wasn't enough. And now, she was afraid he was right: She'd failed.

Outside it had begun to snow, and Mr. Cooper walked to the red truck, opening the passenger side door to get in. Hannah moved slowly, as if in disbelief. How could this have happened? After all the work she'd done, how—with every idea she'd implemented at the museum she'd thought was fulfilling her purpose—how could it all be over?

Heavy with regret and sorrow, she opened the driver's side door and climbed in, prepared to drive Mr. Cooper to the train station.

Not even a few minutes after pulling off, the truck started to rattle and slow down. Hannah turned onto a woodsy road, as the snow had started to pick up a bit. She continued to drive, her thoughts focused on the museum instead of the truck and the weird noises it was now making.

"Now what?" Mr. Cooper asked. "We've barely made it around the corner. Let's go."

She didn't answer him right away, as what she had begun to fear came to fruition. The truck continued to sputter until it eventually stopped. With a groan because this day couldn't possibly get any worse, Hannah dropped her forehead onto the steering wheel.

"The truck can be temperamental," she said, lifting her head up again. "Finicky at times."

"I'm gonna be late for my train, and now the snow is really coming down," Jeb complained.

"It always does for Christmas," she said, looking out the front windshield. That was normally a great thing in Evergreen. Right now she had to admit she was feeling as agitated as Mr. Cooper.

"You've gotta be kiddin' me," Mr. Cooper mumbled, and Hannah followed his gaze.

Through the thick flakes of snow coming down

appeared a man with a white beard, in a red suit, black boots and...

"Ho, ho, ho," he said, coming up to the driver's side of the truck.

Hannah smiled and rolled the window down.

"Do you need help?" the man asked cheerfully.

"No!" Mr. Cooper yelled and Hannah turned to give him a blistering look. "Well, I don't know." Mr. Cooper got out of the truck.

Hannah turned back to the bearded man, who was actually carrying a red velvet sack over his shoulder, just like...With a shake of her head she said, "Yes, we do need help, thank you."

"That truck's old and cranky," the man said as he walked around to the front of the vehicle. "So it sometimes puts up a fight."

Hannah had no idea how he knew this, and had begun to think maybe he'd been hired to dress up for the Christmas Festival. But something about him seemed oddly familiar. Shaking off the thought, she watched as the helpful stranger lifted the hood.

"So if you have a toolbox around..." the man said to Mr. Cooper.

"Never mind," Mr. Cooper replied. "I can handle this myself. I saw a toolbox back at the museum. It'll take me five minutes to walk back there and get it."

Hannah didn't bother to try and stop him. She'd believed what she'd just said about Mr. Cooper in the museum—he was stubborn!

Elliot had arrived at the museum just as Hannah was pulling off in the red truck. He stood there a few moments, thinking he was too late, and then decided to go inside the museum, to see the last touches she'd put on the place. Walking past each exhibit, he couldn't help but smile at how authentic everything looked, and how proud he felt to know the person who was responsible for it all.

He'd been thinking about Hannah nonstop for the past few days, and after talking to her last night at the church, he'd resigned himself to feeling lost and lonely without her for the rest of his life. The Tinker Shop was closed today, as everyone was getting ready for the first night of the festival, but Elliot had stopped by early this morning to pick up some files he needed for a meeting with the foundation. Entering the place this time had felt different, even more so than on the previous days. There was an ominous feeling now, a heaviness that clung to the air even as the bells above the door rang cheerfully. Stepping inside, he closed the door behind him and took a deep steadying breath.

He was just about to walk toward the back office space when something sitting on the counter stopped him. It was a green and white sign surrounded by pine cones. The hand-painted letters on the sign read: The Turner Goods Company. Touching it lightly with his fingers, Elliot smiled as he traced the letters, his chest filling with an indescribable pressure. Beside the sign there was a card with "Happy Holidays" neatly written on the front. Picking up the card, he opened it slowly and read, "Merry Christmas. Love, Hannah."

When had she done this? Had it been before the party at Michelle's? Or after she'd left him at the church? Did it really matter? He shook his head as more questions rolled through his mind. But in the moments that he stood there, Elliot realized none of those questions or the answers he'd been searching for mattered. Not anymore, because he now saw the writing on the wall as plainly as those painted letters on that sign.

He'd wanted to go to Boston to open the second Tinker Shop to prove that he could start a business, be successful and have a family. Something his father had failed at doing. But it had just occurred to him that proving that point didn't matter. Having Jack Lee's validation didn't matter. Especially since the man would likely never know what his son did with his life. His father had never cared before; there was no reason for Elliot to believe that would be any different now. Nor had he even planned to contact his father to let him know. All this time it had been part of a battle Elliot was fighting with himself. One he hadn't realized he would ultimately lose if Hannah wasn't by his side.

Grinning at his own obstinate and foolish thoughts, he searched around for something…anything. He had to show her, tell her how he felt. Grabbing some ribbon lying on the counter and then moving to the shelves to find a red box, he packed it up. Excitement brimmed inside him as he thought of her reaction when she saw the gift. He'd have to think of what to say to her, but he could do that on the ride to the museum to meet her.

Only now, a few minutes after having watched her drive away from the museum, he was alone. Or so he thought.

Elliot could hear a video playing in the movie room and walked closer to see if maybe Hannah had left it on by mistake. He stopped at the entrance to the room the second he saw Jeb staring at the movie screen.

"One last question. What does the Hat Factory mean to you both?"

That was Hannah's voice asking the question, even though she didn't appear on the screen.

"Hmmm, without the Hat Factory there'd be no Evergreen," Jenny Cooper replied.

On the screen, she was seated next to her sister on the same couch Jeb Cooper had just lowered himself down onto.

"It couldn't last forever," Josie said. "Our brother, Jeb, was doing a job none of us wanted."

Elliot could see Jeb's shoulders droop as he watched.

Jenny continued. "Dad would've been so proud that he stepped up. After it closed, the town really had to come together to become more resourceful. And now we're a town that people travel to. That people tell stories about. It goes to show, change is necessary in times of great adversity."

"We were a town built on a wish," Josie said, and then the sisters looked at each other.

"A Christmas wish," they said simultaneously.

Elliot thought about the sisters' last words, and how he'd at one time wished on the snow globe to find true love in Evergreen. Just as he was about to turn away, he noticed Jeb lift a finger to dab at his eyes. Obviously he'd come to some realization, too.

But Elliot didn't stick around to find out what it was. He had to go and find Hannah.

❧

"Everything okay?" the guy dressed like Santa asked, as Hannah leaned against the truck waiting for Mr. Cooper to return with the toolbox.

"No," she replied honestly. "Nothing's okay. Mr. Cooper's leaving without signing. I was trying to help." She looked over at Santa, knowing he couldn't possibly understand what she was talking about, but she needed to say it to someone anyway. "I thought all the hard work I'd put in to the museum would pay off."

"Hannah, you did great," he said. "Sometimes it just takes a little patience."

He turned away before she could ask him what that meant. His words had seemed weirdly cryptic...and oddly familiar. Just as he closed the hood of the truck, another red vehicle pulled up beside it.

"Need a ride?" Josie Cooper asked from the driver's seat of her red Bug.

"No," Hannah replied sadly. "But your brother might in a moment." Jeb Cooper certainly wasn't going to want to ride with her again after this latest debacle.

The Cooper sisters got out of the car.

"Turns out, we can't seem to—" Her words were cut short when Mr. Cooper came walking up.

"I still can't believe that truck runs at all," he said.

That wasn't what Hannah had trouble believing. At this moment she was stunned to see Jeb Cooper smiling. Then she turned, because behind her, the Santa guy had started the truck without any problem.

"But," Jeb continued, as he glanced down at the wrench he'd picked up from the museum. "We're not gonna need it."

The Cooper sisters shrugged, still unsure what was going on. Hannah could relate to that, because she wasn't quite sure what was happening either, especially not when Mr. Cooper walked closer to the truck.

"I see you got the engine started," he said, touching the side of the truck.

"Well," Hannah replied with a shrug. "The truck does what it wants."

"Now, Jeb," Josie began. "We want you to stop this."

"We were driving into town to ask you one last time, just give the nice people what they want," Jenny implored.

Jeb held up his hands to stop his sisters. "I saw the video that Hannah made of you both," he said moving closer to them. "Look, I'm so sorry."

"You did your best," Josie told him.

Jenny chimed in. "What more could anyone ask?"

There was another smile on Mr. Cooper's face and Hannah blinked rapidly to convince herself she wasn't dreaming. Watching the Coopers embrace was the sweetest thing she'd ever seen. And if that was all she got out of this Christmas Eve, that would have to be enough. She was just about to walk around to the driver's side of the truck again, when Mr. Cooper stopped her.

"Ms. Turner, where is the contract?"

"Uh, oh, um." It took a couple seconds for his question to register in her mind, but then she turned around, looking for her bag. The Santa guy appeared right next to her then, holding the clipboard with the contract attached. Surprised didn't quite seem like the right word to describe what she felt at that moment. "Thank you," she said anyway.

With a tentative smile, she handed the clipboard to Mr. Cooper and watched as he slid the pen from the holder on top and began looking at the contract.

"Yes," he said, flipping the first page up. "You keep all the admissions and the gift shop money. That," he continued, scribbling his name on the bottom line, "is as it should be."

Hannah screamed with excitement, clapping her hands before deciding that wasn't enough. She ran to give him a hug. "Thank you so much, Mr. Cooper! Thank you!"

He looked more than a little uncomfortable when she released him, but he tipped his hat to her as his sisters clapped exuberantly beside them. Then Mr. Cooper surprised them all, including probably himself, by taking a tentative step and pulling Hannah into another hug. When they parted this time, he was grinning, and she knew that was his way of telling her he approved of all she'd done. Filled with joy, Hannah hurriedly turned around to thank Santa for all his help, but he was gone.

"Nick," she whispered, only now realizing who Santa had reminded her of.

By nightfall, the Evergreen Christmas Festival and grand opening of the Evergreen Christmas Museum was in full swing. It was still snowing, but only lightly now. All the trees outside the entrance to the museum were lit with white lights. On the other side of the building, red and white tents covered tables of crafts, delicious foods and desserts, drinks and other holiday trinkets for sale. Music played through the loudspeakers—a jazzy rendition of "Jingle Bells."

Hannah was anxious and then elated as she watched Michelle approach. After looking at everything outside the museum, Michelle nodded with approval and leaned in to hug Hannah at the door.

"This is amazing! I love it!" Michelle said, motioning to the giant advent calendar that surrounded the doorway.

"Thanks! I'm so glad you like it. But wait until you see everything else." There was so much to show Michelle, and Hannah was brimming with excitement to hear her comments on every exhibit. She could hardly stop talking as they walked inside together.

The Johansen triplets had agreed to work as hosts for the night, and were dressed in black suits with red bow ties. Hannah and Michelle stopped to greet them and check their coats before going further.

"This is just wonderful, Hannah. You really outdid yourself," Michelle said when they were looking at an exhibit of antique train sets. "Look at all the detail in the summaries above each exhibit."

Hannah knew she was beaming with pride; her cheeks were going to be sore tomorrow from all the smiling she was doing right now. Sonya came over to join them, wearing a lovely black cocktail dress. She held two glasses of champagne and offered one to Michelle. Hannah snagged one from the tray being carried by another one of their volunteer hosts.

"I've never seen anything like this," Sonya said to Michelle and Hannah. "Never even imagined there was a real live Christmas town. But here I am, and now I'm enjoying all this history."

"There's nothing like Christmas in Evergreen," Michelle said to Sonya. "Come on, give it up." The three sisters-to-be touched glasses until they clinked and then took a sip.

"That's exactly the purpose of the museum," Hannah said, her heart so full from the joy she'd seen on everyone's faces. There was no doubt that the museum was a success. One which she'd hoped to share with Elliot.

"People from all around the world are going to enjoy this museum for years to come. Hannah, your parents would be so proud of what you've done here," Michelle said. "I'm so glad I hired you."

With a chuckle Hannah nodded. "I'm glad you did too. Well, you two don't need me to have a good time. I'm gonna walk around to see how everyone else is liking the exhibits."

Really, Hannah just wanted a moment to try and take everything in. The museum was a success and for that she was supremely grateful, but try as she might, she wasn't able to push the thoughts about Elliot aside. The sound of Mr. Cooper's voice did manage to pull her out of that fog of sadness momentarily, and she looked across the room to see him with David and Zoe.

"And this is where the old assembly line was," Mr. Cooper told them, excited to be sharing his experience at the Hat Factory with the next generation. "It'd go right through the stitching room, which is this way."

When they walked past Hannah, all three of them waved, and she grinned at how happy Mr. Cooper now looked. It was wonderful knowing that she'd had a part in bringing him out of the pain of his past.

"You know," she said, walking alongside him. "We could always use someone to give tours at the museum, if you're interested."

"Who knows?" he said with a shrug.

Hannah continued her walk around the place, looking at things as if seeing them for the first time. There was just nothing like this place. She moved her fingers along the heavy red ropes attached to gold posts. They were set up there to keep attendees from getting too close to some of the more fragile displays. When she ended up in the story room, the video was on continuous loop and she stood in the doorway watching Allie, Zoe, Carol and Joe wearing Santa or elf hats on screen.

"And then we ended up moving to Paris," Allie was saying. "And Ryan wanted to wait until he got here to deliver the news, but, you wanna show them?"

Hannah's heart bubbled over with joy as she recalled taping this segment at the last minute yesterday. She'd wondered why Allie had waited so long to get to her story, but once she saw it play out, she knew, and she couldn't have been happier for her longtime friend.

Looking directly at the camera, Allie handed Zoe a picture and continued, "The news is that Zoe is gonna be a big sister. I'm gonna be a mother for the second time, and that means that you mom and dad are gonna be grandparents!"

Zoe had turned around to show the sonogram picture to a very shocked Joe and Carol.

"Oh! My baby! I'm so happy!" Carol screamed, and hugged Allie while Joe looked as if he was going to cry.

Hannah placed a hand over her heart, stifling the tears that threatened to flow as she watched how happy everyone in that video was. There'd been so much more crying and laughing and hugging once she'd turned the camera off, especially when she'd joined in. If anyone deserved to welcome a baby into her new family, it was Allie. And Hannah had sworn to herself late last night that she would only be happy for her friend. Not envious at all.

Besides, her life wasn't over just because Elliot was leaving. And she could still dream about having her own husband and children one day. It wasn't too late for any of that to happen, no matter how much it felt like it was.

Hours after they'd first opened the doors for the museum opening, Hannah stood with her coat buttoned, and stared at the Evergreen mural.

Ezra came up beside her.

"Elliot spent hours trying to get it hung just right," he said.

"It's perfect." No matter how many times she'd seen it, she knew she'd always think the same thing. This duplicate of her parents' famous mural was even more sentimental than the original photo, because Elliot had created it.

"I agree," Ezra said and started to walk away. "Merry Christmas, Hannah."

As she watched him leave, her gaze settled on the tree behind him. This one was decorated in red bulbs, with burlap and brown ornaments, cranberry sprigs and gingham bows. Right there, on a branch close to the top, was a red box that caught her eye. She walked closer, thinking someone must have left it there, because there weren't any others on the tree. Sure, she couldn't remember *every* ornament that had been placed on the twenty-two trees throughout the museum, but something told her this one didn't belong there.

When she settled her attention on the card attached, butterflies danced in her stomach.

"For Hannah. Merry Christmas and congratulations on the museum. Love, Elliot."

She removed the box from the tree and read the card

again before carrying it outside. She had no idea why she didn't open the box right away. Her hands held it tightly as she walked out into the evening air, strolling as if she hadn't a care in the world down Main Street. Everything here was so familiar, and yet still felt so very new. Well, it was actually new for this holiday season. She inhaled deeply, letting the scent of peppermint hot chocolate and fresh-baked cookies fill her senses. There was no place like Evergreen.

With her mind settling on thoughts of the place she called home, she welcomed that comforting feel that Evergreen always offered her. The gazebo was up ahead and she walked toward it, taking a seat on the bench a few feet in front of it.

Sighing heavily, she gave herself a mental pat on the back for a job well done at the museum. Then someone walked by and yelled, "'Night, Hannah!"

"Goodnight!" she shouted back.

For endless moments she sat on that bench, content to people-watch. A family walked by—a mother, father, two kids in between, all holding hands; an older couple hugging and giggling as if they were teenagers; the Cooper sisters who waved and gave a simultaneous, "Merry Christmas!" They were all happy to be living in Evergreen, just as she was, or just as she wanted to be.

With resolve, she finally decided to open the box. How much more painful could it be to receive a gift from the man who was walking out of her life? The man who was also a friend, whom she wanted to be happy, even if it wasn't with her. She pulled the top off and set it on the bench, then reached inside. Emotion filled her with warmth and she gasped when she held the ceramic mitten that was painted to look exactly like the ones she was currently wearing. On top of the mitten was a snowball.

Nervous laughter bubbled up from her chest as she stared down at the most precious gift she'd ever received.

"Presentation is the key to any great gift."

Hannah looked up to see Elliot standing a few feet away. He wore a tan overcoat with a matching scarf. His gloves matched his coat and his jeans were cuffed at the ankles. But none of that mattered. Happiness bloomed inside her at the sight of him.

He walked toward her. "Merry Christmas, Hannah."

"Thank you. It's lovely." She felt like she should say something else, do something else, but she feared there was nothing left to say or do.

His expression was serious, his shoulders set. "I was wondering if you had room for one more story."

"Sure," she said, putting the top on the box and standing. "We can head over to the museum and start the video."

"No," he said and walked over to her. "This is a quick story." He took the box out of her hands and set it on the bench. "It's just for you."

When they were standing, facing each other, he continued. "I fell in love with Hannah Turner from the moment I saw her."

Her cheeks warmed and she glanced away before looking at him once more.

"This Christmas angel fell out of the sky just for me. It took me a while, but no matter what other kinds of things I wanted for myself, Hannah, the main thing I want is you."

"But you wanna go to Boston, and I'm not gonna stand in the way of your dreams," she said, knowing that those were the right words to say. It didn't matter that her heart ached with each one; what mattered was that Elliot be happy in his life. The last thing she wanted was for him to resent her for asking him to stay, when he really wanted to go.

"That was just about asking myself the right questions. I don't need to meet Hannah and Elliot in the city. I know exactly where we are." He took a step closer to her. "That's why I'm keeping the flagship store here, in Evergreen. Sure, it means I'll have to travel to start things up in Boston, but as it turns out, I know someone who's willing to help."

They both looked over to see Ezra walking hand-in-hand with...*Oliver!* No wonder Ezra had been all smiles at the museum tonight. Here Hannah had thought he was just excited about all the exhibits. But no, he was happy to be reunited with Oliver again. She was so happy for them. Ezra smiled and waved. Hannah and Elliot did the same.

"But Elliot," she said, moving closer to him. "I don't want you changing your plans just for me."

"I already did," he said, stopping her next words. "Sometimes, things that seem like they need fixing really don't need fixing at all. I'm with the woman I love. We're part of this town. Why would I want to live anywhere else if it meant being without you?" He put his arms around her, pulling her close. "Hannah, can we try this again?"

If she were writing this story in the book of Evergreen love stories, Hannah couldn't have written a better ending. All she'd ever wanted, all she'd dreamed of was right here in this town and right now, with this man.

"I was hoping you would ask."

When their lips touched this time, it felt like the first time. Even better, Hannah thought as she leaned in closer, loving the feel of Elliot holding her and replaying his words about their being a part of this town in her mind.

Epilogue

It was finally time for Hannah and Elliot to sit down and tell their story for the record. But since it was Christmas and the museum was closed, they'd set up the video camera and backdrop and began recording right there in Michelle's living room.

"Even in Evergreen," she said to the camera, "things are gonna change. And sometimes, with just a little patience, you realize you're gonna have to let change happen. And that may mean letting go of a few things."

"Or adding a few things," Elliot added, and then looked at her with a grin. When he returned his attention to the camera, he continued. "The point is, change is more fun if you get creative."

"And work together," she added.

His arm was around her and he rubbed her arm. "Keeping some traditions, of course."

"Oh, yeah, like snowball fights." She grinned with the memory.

"Christmas baking."

"Gingerbread houses."

"Mmmmm."

"Christmas movies," she continued.

He tilted his head and grinned at her. "Tinkering."

"I'm so glad you changed the name of the shop."

He shrugged and hugged her closer. "Out with the old."

"Time to eat!" Michelle yelled, and David stopped taping the video.

Hannah and Elliot got up and went to join the others at the table. They were all having dinner at Michelle's house this year. She and Gordon had fixed a ton of food, and most of it was on the large dining room table waiting for them to indulge.

There was a delectable-looking baked turkey, and the baked ham was prepared just the way Hannah's mother used to, with slices of pineapple, cloves and cherries. Also on the table were bowls filled with sweet potatoes, collard greens, baked macaroni and cheese and so much more.

Hannah and Elliot went to take their seats at one of the tables and she waved at Henry, who'd also decided to join them, and was sitting between Gordon and Sonya. On the other side sat Bea, Michelle and David. Before any food was eaten, Gordon had them all join hands and bow their heads as he took them into a prayer of thanksgiving. Hannah listened intently, remembering her father doing the same thing at all their holiday meals, and imagining that this time next year, Elliot would be at the head of the table in their home, taking up this same tradition. By the time the prayer ended, she was filled with joy, and eagerly joined in when Bea suggested a toast.

"To love, happy endings, and new beginnings!"

The End

Maple Sweet Potato Gratins with Ginger Pecan Streusel

Prep Time: 15 mins.
Cook Time: 90 mins.
Serves: 12

Ingredients

- 4 medium-large sweet potatoes, scrubbed clean
- 4 tablespoons butter, melted
- ¼ cup maple syrup
- As needed coarse-ground salt and black pepper
- 4 tablespoons flour
- ¼ cup brown sugar
- ½ cup coarsely chopped pecans
- 2 teaspoons crystalized ginger, fine chopped
- ¼ cup butter, melted

Preparation

1. Preheat oven to 400°F. Butter 12 small individual-sized baking dishes and reserve.
2. Pierce sweet potatoes with a fork; transfer to baking sheet. Bake uncovered for about 60 to 90 minutes or until very tender.
3. Slice cooked sweet potatoes in half; scoop out tender sweet potato and transfer to a food processor bowl fitted with a steel blade. Add butter and maple syrup; process until completely smooth. Add salt and black pepper; taste and adjust flavor.
4. Reduce oven temperature to 350°F. Transfer whipped sweet potatoes to buttered baking dishes.
5. Combine flour, brown sugar, pecans and ginger in small bowl; add melted butter and stir until mixture resembles coarse crumbs. Sprinkle evenly over the top of each baking dish.
6. Arrange baking dishes on sheet pans; bake for

15 minutes or until streusel topping is lightly browned.

Thanks so much for reading
Christmas in Evergreen: Bells Are Ringing.
We hope you enjoyed it!

You might like these other books from Hallmark
Publishing:

Christmas in Evergreen
Christmas in Evergreen: Letters to Santa
Christmas in Evergreen: Tidings of Joy
A Gingerbread Romance
Mistletoe in Juneau
On Christmas Avenue
Wrapped Up in Christmas Hope

For information about our new releases and exclusive offers, sign up for our free newsletter at
hallmarkchannel.com/hallmarkpublishing-newsletter

You can also connect with us here:

Facebook.com/HallmarkPublishing

Twitter.com/HallmarkPublish

About the Author

Lacey Baker, a Maryland native, lives with her husband, three children, grandson and an English Bulldog in what most would call suburban America—a townhouse development where everybody knows each other and each other's kids. Family cookouts, reunion vacations, and growing up in church have all inspired Lacey to work towards her dreams and to write about the endurance of family and the quest to find everlasting love.

Her previous books include *A Gingerbread Romance* for Hallmark Publishing. She's written in several genres, including small town romance, YA paranormal (as Artist Arthur), a cozy mystery series titled Rumors, and adult paranormal (as A.C. Arthur).

Turn the page for a sneak preview of

Mistletoe in Juneau

by Dahlia Rose!

Chapter One

Even before Halloween jack-o'-lanterns came down and the Thanksgiving turkey was carved, New York City came alive with holiday magic. Twinkling lights and decorations graced the store windows in Manhattan, and at Rockefeller Center, the massive tree made the perfect centerpiece for Christmas in a city whose buildings reached for the sky. By the time New Yorkers heard the first merry jingle of bells or the hearty laugh of a mall Santa, they were in the Christmas spirit.

Thirty-year old Danni St. Peters loved the city. A Brooklyn girl born and raised, she could get from Canarsie to Clinton Hills by bus or train, and she always knew which street had the latest fashions or the hottest new restaurant. She'd built her career around that adventurous spirit and had made a name for herself. *Danni On the Run*, her video channel, had over two million subscribers—and that wasn't even counting all her other followers on social media. She was well known across the country and going worldwide.

"We're ready for you on set, Danni." The producer

of the morning show segment, a young woman wearing a headset, looked in the room as the makeup artist made sure Danni's face was flawless.

Danni met the producer's gaze in the mirror with a wink. "Thanks a bunch!"

"You look marvelous," a male voice added. "Are you ready to wow them with that Danni pizzazz?"

Austin Hammond, who had accompanied her to the morning show, stood at the door. His smile traveled to his eyes, making the blue even warmer. As always, Austin was dressed to the nines. His champagne-colored sweater was paired with dark dress pants and expensive, on-trend shoes. He'd left the jacket in the greenroom.

"Ready as I'll ever be," she said.

"Big smile." He made a smile motion with his hand, and Danni gave him a rueful shake of her head. Then she put a bright smile on and followed the producer down the hall.

Today she had an appearance on the entertainment channel's best-rated daytime show. Being featured on *The Aisha White Show* was another step up in her career. Aisha was a daytime drama actress whose career had taken off, and now she had her own line of clothes and shoes as well as the talk show.

Danni caught a glimpse of herself in one of the lighted mirrors offstage. Two barrettes pulled her hair back from her face to accent her cheekbones. Light bronzer made her teak-colored skin glow, like she'd just come from a beach in the Caribbean.

Danni stepped from the hallway into the shots of the

cameras. When the lights hit her, she came alive. The audience clapped as she ran down the walkway, giving high fives and taking a selfie or two with guests before bounding up the two small steps that led to the stage.

"Danni, you look fabulous!" Aisha's bright eyes were kind and caught the lights of the set, and her wide smile instantly put Danni at ease.

"White pantsuit in winter—brave girl!" Aisha held out her arms for an embrace.

"You look amazing yourself, Aisha. That red dress is perfect on you, and I'm jealous." Danni hugged her lightly while they exchanged air kisses, and then did a little twirl. "I'm not a Hamptons girl, Aisha. We Brooklyn girls live a bit fashion-dangerously. Besides, I paired it with your red pumps and the look is fierce."

"Yes, yes, it's perfect." The audience clapped their approval while she and the host got seated on a pair of comfortable plush chairs.

"Danni St. Peters," Aisha said with warmth. "Your name is on everyone's lips. You have millions of followers who just eat up your every adventure. Tell us how it started."

Danni smiled. "It started because I was a dreamer. I didn't just want to read about places in a book—I wanted to experience them. So, three years ago, after saving for two years before that, I took my first trip to Paris… on a budget. And let me tell you, visiting Paris, surviving on croissants and cheese, and exploring the city was the best time I ever had. I stayed in a low-rent hotel, I made videos and livestreamed the different places I visited, and people loved it because they could relate."

Aisha said, "And you've gone much further than that. *Danni on The Run* is food, it's dancing…I loved the one when you tried hot yoga for the first time. Oh! And the food truck Friday in Charlotte, where you ate that loaded mac and cheese."

Danni threw her head back and laughed. "The food in that town is so decadent. *Danni On the Run* is going back for a second trip there for something called Queen Charlotte day, so look out for that in February."

Aisha leaned forward conspiratorially. "What about the man in Danni's life?"

Danni swallowed uncomfortably and looked toward backstage. What should she call Austin these days? They had morphed from manager and client to couple, and she honestly didn't know when it had happened. Now he practically beamed…and before Danni could say a thing, Austin jogged out waving at the audience.

Dude! she thought. *This is not your interview!*

But she tucked away her irritation, because as always, Austin didn't mean any harm in his actions. He was just…*excitable?* Yeah, that was the word.

He was the quintessential New York man, from the top of his blond head down to the loafers on his feet. His smile was perfect—white even teeth. Danni almost expected the little sparkle she saw in toothpaste ads. And Austin Hammond was accustomed to being in front of an audience. His family vacationed in Martha's Vineyard and played racquetball with the elite. He had tickets to all the best events, and he'd hinted they would need to coordinate their outfits for New York Fashion Week next year.

"Austin Hammond," Aisha said. "We all know who you are, and now we see why you have that gleam in your eyes."

With his hands placed on Aisha's shoulders, Austin kissed her on both cheeks. As he sat down in the chair next to Danni and held her hand, the host continued. "When did you guys meet?"

Danni opened her mouth to answer, but Austin beat her to the punch. "I met the lovely Danni last year at the Harlem Wine Festival. I saw her, and I knew she was the one."

Am I? And was Austin really the one for her? Even as confusion filtered through her mind, Danni kept her smile pasted firmly on her face.

"So, love at first sight, hmmm?" Aisha turned to her audience. "And they said romance was dead."

The rest of the interview consisted of Danni answering questions when she could. Austin also touted being her manager and anything else he could get out before the interview was over. She was tired by the end of it.

"That went wonderfully," Austin said, once they were offstage and heading toward the exit.

"It went," Danni murmured.

He frowned. "Not happy with it, honey?"

She cast a sidelong glance at him. "Well, you did all the commentary. You tell me."

"I gave the audience what they wanted." Austin grinned. "We are building your brand."

"I'm not a puppet. Austin, I can speak for myself," Danni said firmly. "It was my brand before you stepped in, and it will continue to be so."

"Don't be mad, babe, it went great," he said and patted out a little beat on his leg.

He never listens.

But he was only trying to help, she told herself. She was running on fumes—no food and plenty of caffeine—and it was making her oversensitive. She should quit being so hard on the guy.

She pasted a smile on her face as they stepped outside. "It went great. I'm just a bit tired. It's been a whirlwind of a year, and I honestly need a break."

"Ah-ah-ah, not the 'b' word again," Austin said.

A sleek black town car pulled up, and the driver came around to help her in. When they were settled in the back seat, he spoke again.

"This went fantastic. Did you see how they practically got out of their seats when I came out? It's what they want, babe—the most eligible, handsome man on your arm."

Danni said nothing as the car pulled away from the curb. Austin kept talking while she half-listened.

She was going to every event, every weekend—new restaurant openings, shows, clubs. When she'd first started out, she'd been able to choose what she did, but since he'd become her manager, she hadn't said no to a single invite. She no longer got her videos out after one simple edit. Now, it was tweak and re-tweak, take and re-take to get the perfect shot. The organizers who invited her wanted to be showcased in the best light.

Some of the clubs were not her scene. They were loud, hot, and crass, where egos were built on how someone dressed— usually, the more scantily, the better. That wasn't her.

She missed the days when it was just about her bucket list. The brochure for the butterfly exhibit she wanted to visit was still on her desk. Danni smiled, thinking about when she could actually go sit and film while butterflies flitted all around. Maybe they'd land on her hands or shoulders...

"Danni... Danni, are you listening to me?" Austin took her hand and patted it in concern. "Do you need to eat? Low blood sugar and Danni St Peters do not mix."

"Sorry," Danni apologized. "Slight headache. You're right though, I haven't had anything to eat since breakfast."

"I have protein bars, or should we stop and get you a quick sandwich? Danni, you need to take care of you, too," Austin said with worry in his voice. "You have to be on the ball. You still have that meeting for the makeup brand. If you get this campaign, you'll be worldwide baby, so you have to think about when you eat."

"Okay, Austin. I'll handle it... I know you're trying to help, but right now it's a bombardment of words." Danni sighed and leaned forward to tap the glass barrier between them and the driver. "Charles, can you take me to the Renaissance Hotel, please?"

"Yes ma'am." The driver made a left turn at the light.

"You don't have to see them until noon, and I can

go with you." Austin smiled and picked up her hand to kiss it. "You need me to work this deal for you, honey."

Danni gently removed her hand. "Austin, I did this by myself before we met last year. Thank you, but this one I can manage on my own. I'm going to grab a quick lunch…alone, then freshen up for the meeting."

"Will I see you tonight?" His tone was subdued.

She shook her head. "I need to shop for my family get-together and go home to wrap gifts. I'll see you Sunday for dinner, how's that?"

He brightened. "I'll get Salvador to make us something fantastic at Ciao's."

Danni nodded. "Sounds perfect."

"Oh, that other show called, *The Scoop*. They still want you for next week."

"No. I won't be anywhere near that guy. He demeans people, and he glorifies misery. Don't even respond, and he'll go away."

"But—"

"*No*," Danni cut him off firmly. "I won't be fodder for his rumor mill."

Austin took her hand in his. "You're right, of course. That's not the image you're going for. I'll ask the street team for input."

When had she gotten a street team? Shouldn't she have heard about that? Still, she warmed pleasantly at his support. It wasn't usual for him to follow her direction when it came to her career, so it was wonderful when he listened and turned on his boyish charm.

"That's great," she said. "Thank you for seeing my

point of view."

The car pulled to a stop outside the hotel, and she gathered her purse and the satchel that carried her laptop, tablet, and even a tripod in case she was inspired to shoot something interesting for her show.

She kissed him on the cheek. "See you Sunday. Go visit your parents, take them a gift."

Austin laughed. "Danni, you are so innocent sometimes. We haven't exchanged gifts since I was fourteen. They can literally buy anything they want."

She shook her head at his response. He blew her a kiss as the car pulled away.

Danni took a huge breath, clearing her lungs with the cold winter air, then walked toward the hotel and went directly to the posh restaurant on the bottom floor. The truth was, she could've seen him before her family's holiday get-together.

The dinner always happened early because her parents spent the holiday in Florida. It was the luxury they spent the entire year saving up for: a month in a warm climate to get away from the New York chill. This year, Danni had the perfect gift for them. Their month would be spent in a luxury condo instead of the cramped timeshare with two other couples her mother always complained about.

The waitress came over with a smile. "Good afternoon. Lunch menu?"

"Please," Danni said gratefully. "Can I have the molten hot chocolate, extra warm, please?"

"And extra whipped cream?" the waitress hinted.

"It's perfect to beat the cold."

"That sounds amazing. Put me down for that."

She studied the menu while waiting for her drink. The first time she'd tasted the hot chocolate at the hotel, she'd been surprised to learn it had red wine in the recipe. She'd loved the idea so much, she'd done a livestream with the chef as he made his signature winter drink. He explained how the heat evaporated the alcohol content of the wine, leaving only a rich flavor that enhanced the chocolate.

The waitress was quick to return with her beverage and Danni ordered the salmon burger with steak fries for lunch. After the first delicious sip, she impulsively pulled out her phone and started to record.

"Have you ever just missed reading by a window while the rain falls? Or going thrift shopping for that perfect pair of retro jeans? Lunch in the park with girl-friends, watching cute guys play Frisbee or flag football? I miss that. Sometimes the glitz and glamour takes away from the small things," she said into the camera. "Even this drink right now…it should be shared with someone who wants to snuggle up next to a fire, or watch a movie at home wearing mismatched socks." Danni gave a soft laugh. "Or maybe I'm just crazy, and I should be grateful for what I have?"

Read the rest!
Mistletoe in Juneau is available now.